W9-CBG-253

THE MYSTERY COTTAGE IN LEFT FIELD

THE MYSTERY COTTAGE IN LEFT FIELD

by Remus F. Caroselli

G. P. Putnam's Sons
New York

Published simultaneously in Canada by
Longman Canada Limited, Toronto.
PRINTED IN THE UNITED STATES OF AMERICA
10 up

Library of Congress Cataloging in Publication Data
Caroselli, Remus F
The mystery cottage in left field.
SUMMARY: In the spring of 1929, 12-year-old Jimmy makes friends with the new woman in his Providence, R.I., neighborhood and becomes involved with gangsters who have been searching for her son for a year.
[1. Gangs—Fiction] I. Title.
PZ7.C22My 1979 [Fic] 78-24368
ISBN 0-399-20672-8

To
Gen,
Anne, Diane and Tom

Chapter One

Early in 1929 I turned twelve, but spring just didn't seem to want to come around that year. My friends all thought it was my love of baseball that made me keep repeating, "I wish Providence was as warm as Florida!" But my feelings had nothing to do with the cold Rhode Island weather. I guess I must have done a pretty good job of hiding my cowardice from them. What they didn't know was that I was praying for the baseball season to begin because I was hoping it would put an end to those stupid, scary games we had been forced to play since the middle of February.

A terrible thing had happened that year on St. Valentine's Day. In a garage in Chicago six gangsters had been machine-gunned down in cold blood by a rival gang. I admit I was really excited reading about it in *The Providence Journal* and listening to stories of Bugsy Moran and Al Capone on the radio. But Roy Oates and Eats Farrell, they just couldn't ever stop talking about it! They were the biggest guys in our gang on Plympton Street, and they were pretty clever at inventing new games. This made them our leaders, except in baseball.

In baseball they were so clumsy I enjoyed watching them fumble a ball or strike out. In the same way, I guess, they got their kicks during the rest of the year watching us smaller guys trying to puff ourselves up to their size. The truth was that baseball made me feel almost equal to them.

Just as we expected, right after the St. Valentine's Day news was out, Roy and Eats had us becoming bootleggers and hijackers and G-men. At first I really enjoyed the games they dreamed up, even though they always ended up the same way, with most of us being massacred against the back wall of Aldo Russo's chicken coop, which we used as our clubhouse.

It wasn't long before Roy started to throw his weight around, and he had it to throw, believe me! I bet he weighed twice as much as I did. He was strong as an ox, looked like one as a matter of fact, except that he had black curly hair and the fattest and reddest face you've ever seen. He was always one of the gangsters, and I could never understand that, because he could have been anything he wanted to be in those games.

To me nothing can beat being one of the good guys, the G-men. It was always a nice feeling to win as a good guy; but when you win as a bad guy, well, I just never felt right about that. But not old Roy! He made darn sure the good guys never won, anyway. He always chose lanky old Eats Farrell to be on his side, because Eats was the only one of us big enough to challenge him. Funny thing was that we had three sides, with one set of bad guys, the hijackers, and the good guys always ending up together against that wall, while the gangsters, whooping and cheering, mowed them all down.

It got pretty rough after a while. Roy was the bully of Plympton Street, and it didn't take long for this new power to go to his head. Soon there was no choosing of sides at all. You went where Roy wanted you to go. He and Eats and the Lanni brothers and a few of the nastier younger kids became a permanent team. You couldn't say you didn't want to play the crazy game, either, because he and his gang would round up anyone who set foot on the street after school whether you were playing or not. A guy could be coming back from a trip to the grocery store and suddenly find himself being shoved into that dark chicken coop along with the other captured ones. He'd be pushed and jabbed into place along the wall, and there were some mighty ugly bruises and cuts handed out. What was bad was that the little guys on Roy's team became as mean as he was, kicking shins and elbowing in the dark, and a lot of ill feeling developed among us, so much so that I began to wonder whether we'd be able to put together a Plympton Street baseball team that spring.

It was Eats Farrell who kept things from really getting out of hand. Although he was big and liked to show off, especially when it came to telling us how much he knew about sex, he could never really be mean. Several times he found the guts to stand up to Roy when he was doing something nasty like twisting somebody's leg nearly out of its joint in a toehold, and he made the big bully ease off. I often wished I had some of Eats's guts. I think that's what bothered me most. Even more than the painful shots to the ribs that Roy would sometimes give me as he forced me to the rear of that chicken coop, I hated having to admit to myself that I just didn't have the courage to stand up against his bullying.

It's easy to see, then, why I was so happy when baseball season began to roll around. Try as he might, Roy couldn't keep his regulars from deserting him, especially the Lanni brothers. They led the way. They lived for baseball, Skinny the fastest base runner I've ever played with, and Tony a second baseman who could cover the whole infield. Of course, Aldo Russo, who hoped to be pitching for LaSalle Academy a year from then and for Providence College four years later, was right with them along with Brian Coughlin, who was Aldo's closest pal. It took no special bravery for the rest of us to fall right in, and soon old Roy and Eats were feeling a bit of their own weaknesses on the old sandlot down by the brook on Pleasant Valley Parkway.

On the Saturday my sister Agnes was born, I couldn't get down to that ball field fast enough. I was awakened earlier than usual by the sound of moaning coming from my parents' room. As I raised my head from my pillow, I saw my five-year-old brother, Dennis, sitting up in the bed next to mine, his big blue eyes full of tears.

"It's Mamma!" he cried. I listened again to the painful sound from the other room. Panic came over me. Women could die giving birth!

I rushed to the bedroom door and looked down the hall, Dennis by my side, clinging to my pajama leg. The door of my parents' room was closed. I heard footsteps on the stairway. At the top of the stairs my father's head appeared, black beard unshaven, hair wild and soaked with sweat, his blue eyes looking as frightened as Dennis's. My stomach flipped and I shuddered. "Mamma?" I asked, gulping down the huge lump in my throat.

My father signaled us to be quiet and follow him downstairs. We passed my mother's door, the sound of her heavy breathing making my insides tremble. Downstairs my father said, "Aunt Mabel's here already. She's making breakfast. The midwife is on the way to help your mother. There's nothing to worry about. In a little while we'll have another Loughlin, maybe a little brother or sister. Now, go in and have a nice big breakfast. Then, Jimmy, you help Dennis get dressed and take him along to the ball field with you for a while." He patted my shoulder. "Nothing to worry about, boy. Your mother's going to be all right."

I looked up at him and swallowed hard. His eyes did not seem as sure as his words. Who was he kidding? He was as frightened as I was! And he was guilty, too! He had caused that torment in my mother's stomach. He had placed her life in danger, and he knew it. What he didn't know was that I knew it, too. I knew all about how babies got there. And at this moment I hated him for it.

My mother's sister already had hot oatmeal on the table for us when we entered the kitchen door. She had left our two-year-old, Bobby, at home with Uncle Bob and their own three kids. She tried to smile, but I could tell she was feeling as sick about the whole thing as I was. My mother's moaning seemed to be growing louder. None of us felt like eating except Dennis. He was already spooning his cereal.

"It might have been better if she had gone to the Lying-In," Aunt Mabel said, wincing. "This one seems to be harder than the others for her."

I watched the back of my father's neck redden. I knew he was angry, but he kept his voice low. "She had no trouble with the others," he said. "Mrs. McGinn did all right by her then, and she'll be all right now. You're forgetting the big epidemic of impetigo they had in that hospital. I'm not risking infection of my family! Besides, I don't believe in mass-produced babies!"

Aunt Mabel shrugged. She should have known how dead set he had always been against babies being born in hospitals. The whole neighborhood had been excited a couple of years ago when The Lying-In was being built down along Pleasant Valley Parkway, not too far from where we played ball, but I remembered how he had preached against it then. "Production lines are okay for machines," he'd say, "but babies need the warmth of a family around them."

I remembered it clearly, because it was around that time that I first began to find out how babies really were born. We used to go down to watch the workers putting up the huge brick building which was to be the "baby factory," as my father used to call it.

I couldn't eat, but this was one morning my father didn't notice, for he couldn't himself. He didn't even wait for Dennis to empty his bowl before he stood up and said, "Now, Jimmy, we men won't do much good around here. Mrs. McGinn will be here any moment to look after your mother. You keep Dennis with you until noon, then come by the garage and we'll all come home to lunch together. By then we'll be able to meet the new member of the Loughlin family."

He seemed even more anxious to get away from there than I was. The big he-man, he was always preaching to me to do the manly thing, and here he was, now, as cowardly as I was! I think the only thing he ever approved about me was the way I hit a baseball. That made him proud, but as for other things— He could never understand why I loved to read so much. He owned the Texaco gasoline station at the corner of our street, and he was always after me to become interested in motors. He thought Roy Oates was the greatest kid in the world because Roy loved helping my father take cars apart and put them together again. He just had a natural talent for all mechanical things, he and Brian Coughlin.

I think my father resented my size, too. He would much rather have had me as rugged and athletic as Aldo Russo or as big as Roy and Eats, even clumsy as they were. Once, after my father had punished me for spending too much time in the Sprague House Library instead of helping him sweep out his repair station as he had asked me to do, I told my mother about all these doubts I had about my father. She laughed. "Your father loves you," she said. "Someday you'll understand that no two people see things alike. That has nothing to do with love. Just remember that whether it seems right or wrong to you, that whatever he does or says to you, he does because he thinks it's best for you. You're very precious to him."

On this particular Saturday I just couldn't get away from him and my mother's cries fast enough. Dennis and I ran back upstairs, Mother's sounds driving us faster as we passed her door. I helped my little brother dress, put on my own play clothes, then dashed back down those steps and outside, heading for Pleasant Valley Parkway.

When we reached the corner of our street, who should be rounding it but old Mrs. McGinn, looking plump and cheerful as ever and carrying her little brown valise. What terrible, mysterious instruments lay within that bag? I couldn't keep my eyes off it as she spoke to us. "Oh, here they are, my two precious Loughlin babies! My, how they've grown! Well, in a while we'll have a little baby sister for you." She seemed a bit out of breath. I looked up into her smiling face, which was glowing with sweat.

"A sister?" I asked softly.

"That's how I'm betting this time," she said. "Wouldn't you like a beautiful little sister? Now, don't worry, Jimmy. Everything is going to be fine. Your mother is a young, strong woman."

"She's in pain," I said, choking on the words.

"It won't be long, child. It was the same way with you and with young Dennis here and little Bobby. Think how proud she'll be to have another like you three!" She put her hand on my shoulder. "There's nothing she's prouder of in this world, son, I can tell you that." I sniveled and shrugged. "Go along now and play.

There'll be a sister waiting when you get back home. And a happy mother."

I began to feel better after that. After all, who would know better than Mrs. McGinn? She had delivered almost half the babies in the Mt. Pleasant section of Providence. By the time I got to the field and heard the crack of the ball against the bat, most of my fears were gone.

Chapter Two

In the spring before we got our neighborhood teams all set for the summer season, Saturday was always my favorite day. For then we would have a game of Rotation baseball going from early morning until suppertime, non-stop.

We were never short of the eleven men we needed, nine in the field and two at bat. If you got to the field a little late, you didn't mind waiting for your turn to play, because before long someone would have to leave the game to go home to do some chore or other. Besides, there were always a half-dozen or so guys around who would be happy to play jack-knife with you or just tell stories. Sometimes, some of us even took in the Saturday afternoon cowboy serial at the Castle Theater and made it back to the ball field for a couple of more hours' play.

What I liked most about Rotation was that we didn't just play with our own Plympton gang. Guys from Fallon Avenue and Berlin Street and upper Academy Avenue would join us. That way we could size one another up before summer vacation when each neighborhood in Mt.

Pleasant would have its own team to compete with the others. It was a nice feeling, with a lot of kidding and laughing and no pressure, and it gave us a chance to try out in every position in baseball. It worked like this. As a batter was put out, he would take his place in left field and then each player would move up to the next position, rotating around the outfield, then the infield, up to pitcher and catcher and finally to batter.

That morning I got to the field early enough to be one of the starters. My position was center field. We had to wait a couple of minutes for the eleventh man, but when Aldo Russo showed up, we were under way in no time at all. I took my little brother's hand. I didn't want to leave him by home plate because that was too near the road, and I knew he'd be tempted to cross it to go play in the brook. Cars really sped along that parkway. So I took him out to center field with me and told him to go sit down behind me by the white picket fence that surrounded the little white cottage with blue shutters that faced both left and center fields.

My mother had always admired this house, with its big yard and beautiful gardens. But the place mystified her, she said. Although it was always so neat and well-tended, she had never seen a living soul either go in or come out of it. Even when I had told her that I had seen a woman there, she didn't seem convinced, because I could never describe the lady.

I had only seen her two or three times, and then for just a second or so as she entered the house from the backyard. That morning the yard looked more beautiful than ever, with the lilac bushes in bloom at both the near and far corners of the fence and the bright pink azaleas just peeking over from the center of the garden and the golden forsythia behind that.

Roy Oates's loud, croaking voice brought me back to the game. "Awright out there! Wake up! First batter's up!" Even here, where he should have been hanging his head in shame for his lack of skill, he could not help trying to be the big boss. He was the catcher, and poor old long, stringy Eats, who couldn't put one over the plate if he carried the ball there, was the pitcher. Skinny Lanni was batting. Eats's long arms went into what was supposed to be a wind-up but looked more like a couple of hockey sticks being flung in the air. The ball shot out and was sailing right for Skinny's head. But Skinny was too fast. He scrambled out of the way, and, of course, Roy's catcher's mitt was nowhere near the ball, and it flew past him, out of the lot and across the road and into the brook.

While we waited for the ball to be retrieved, I looked back to see what Dennis was doing. To my surprise, there was a woman standing inside the picket fence looking out at us. This time I could really see her. She was tall and very thin and dark, dressed in a violet-colored dress. Her hair was caught up on the top of her head in a strange-looking bun, and what looked like a silver comb glistened in it. As I watched, I saw her lean over the fence and look down at where my little brother was sitting. Dennis turned and looked up at her, and judging from the way his head began to nod, he began to talk away at her a mile a minute.

She'd been living there for almost a year now, and

it was the first time that I, or anyone else for that matter, had ever seen her in full view. I was tempted to go up a little closer to get even a better look, but Roy's annoying commands were calling us back to the game.

This time Eats, at the mound again, knew enough to just lob the ball over easy. Even at that, Skinny had to take a couple of steps to meet it. He whacked it a good one, and it came flying out high over the second baseman's head, and I had to turn and run back to keep up with it. This brought me quite close to the fence. As I reached for the ball, I just couldn't keep my eyes from going for a split second to the striking face of that lady. It was just long enough, though, for me to misjudge the ball and have to bounce off the end of my glove. Aldo Russo was right there to recover for me, but by the time the ball got back to home plate, that speed demon of a Skinny Lanni had beat it all around the bases for a home run. You should have heard that Roy Oates scream at me then!

I wouldn't have minded anyone else making fun of me, but that clumsy fool—heck, he wouldn't have even known the ball had gone past him! Funny thing, though, it didn't bother me for long that morning, because I began to think about that woman again. That face— It sort of reminded me of the Mona Lisa that Sister Margaret tried to explain to us in Art Appreciation. There was a tenderness there as she smiled down at my little brother, but there was a sadness, too. Those dark eyes seemed to hold so many secrets. Funny, how from just one glance I could feel so many things. That woman was sad and she was hurt and she was lonely—I was sure of it. I began to wonder if she lived there in that cottage all by herself. Maybe her husband was dead. And all her kids, too.

All through the game, as I worked my way up out of the outfield to the infield, then to pitching and catching and finally to bat, I kept imagining all sorts of tragedies that might have happened to that poor lady.

Aldo Russo and I were at bat together, and we stayed up there for a long time that morning. We were both hitting the ball a country mile. Twice I was delighted to whiz it right through Roy Oates's big fat legs and to listen to all the little guys hooting at him.

When I finally popped out, I took my pace in left field and looked up at the sun. It was getting pretty late. I wondered if my little sister had been born yet, and if my mother was still in pain. Mrs. McGinn had seemed so confident about everything. Even about it being a girl. I called out to second base to Lucky Murphy for the right time. Lucky was the only one with a watch. His father was pretty rich, owned a couple of drugstores. "Ten-thirty," Lucky said. I figured I'd have time to work my way up to bat again before going to the garage to meet my father.

I looked back to see how Dennis was doing with his new friend, but he was alone now, sitting with his back against the fence. My eyes searched the yard. She was not there, either. She must have gone back into the house. I found myself feeling sorry for her. She had seemed so lonely.

Aldo was still up. I knew he was due to hit a long one

to this field. And he did, on the very next pitch. This time I caught it, a magnificent catch, if I must say so myself. I had to reach back over my head to get it. Eat your heart out, Roy Oates!

By the time I had worked my way up to second base, I noticed the lady had returned. Dennis was once more gabbing over the fence with her, and then I saw her give him something. When a fly ball fell between Aldo and me in short center field, Aldo said to me, "Hey, that lady over there must be Italian. She just gave your brother a piece of pizza. I can smell it all the way over here."

I sneaked another peak at Dennis and he was sitting with his back to the fence again, munching happily away. He had always loved pizza from the very first time he had tasted it with me at Aldo's house. Aldo's mother made the best pizza in the world, and all the Irish kids in the neighborhood (Mt. Pleasant was nearly all Irish then) were nuts about it and would swap Aldo all sorts of things for it. There were a few, though, who were afraid to try it, afraid of that spicy foreign stuff.

I guess I was that way myself at first, until Aldo's sister, Laura, kind of teased me into taking the first bite. Laura was younger than Aldo, nearer my age, and she was a beauty. As a matter of fact, she's the first one I thought of when Sister Margaret discussed the Mona Lisa. Only I thought Laura was more beautiful. So Aldo's mentioning the pizza set me to daydreaming about Laura.

I had been doing an awful lot of that during that week. Father Simmons had even had to caution me in confession to try to think about girls less and to play more sports and keep busy. What he didn't know was that it was always the same girl that I had those thoughts about and that they came to me even in the middle of a game like this.

Skinny Lanni was at the plate again, and the crack of the bat woke me too late to be able to handle his hot grounder. Roy whooped with joy as I bobbled it. I forced myself to keep my mind on the game. I didn't look out toward the cottage again until I came to bat. Dennis seemed to still be talking away to the lady. I wondered what in the world a five-year-old could talk about for so long. My mother always said Dennis must have kissed the Blarney somehow.

I guess my mind really couldn't stay on the game that morning, because I popped out on the very first pitch. It was almost time to go to my father, anyway. Joey Scully of the Fallon Avenue bunch took my slot, and I trotted out past center field to go pick up my brother. Of course, I had told no one what was going on at home.

When I got to the fence, the lady was standing there with a huge bouquet of lilacs, forsythia, and dogwood blossoms in her arms. She smiled, and though her dark eyes did not lose their sadness, there was a warmth about her face that made me like her right away.

"You luke like you' broder," she said, nodding.

I didn't know what to say. I shrugged. She was foreign, all right. She sounded something like Aldo's mother. Then there was that pizza smell still rising from my brother. So I guessed she was Italian. She seemed much older than I had thought, older than my mother, maybe even as old as Grandma Loughlin.

"You' mamma have new baby today?" she asked.

My face must have become a huge flame. I nodded in embarrassment. So that's what blabbermouth Dennis had been gabbing about!

She held out the big bouquet to me. "Dees for you' mamma," she said.

"Thank you," I said, swallowing hard and taking the flowers.

"I 'ope you fin' nice girla at 'ome, pretty like you two!" she said, beaming.

I felt my face get even hotter. I nodded again. I had an urge to turn and run and to call after Dennis to come with me, but there was so much kindness on that face, and loneliness, too, like she wanted to follow us home. I knew I just *had* to say *something.* I cleared my throat. My voice stuck a bit, but I finally got the words out. "My mother loves flowers. They'll help her. Thank you so much!"

She nodded, pleased by my words. I took my brother's hand, but before we could turn to go, she said, "My boy, he play baseball a lot."

This stopped me. So she wasn't alone. She had a son. Funny, we never saw him. I don't know why I didn't ask her where her son was then. I really wanted to know. I guess it was just something in her face, the sadness maybe. "It's my favorite game," I said, then while I tried to think of what to say next, she tousled my brother's hair and said good-bye.

I gave Dennis the flowers to carry. I didn't want Roy asking questions as we crossed the field again.

"I'll come back tomorrow," Dennis called back to the lady over his shoulder.

I looked back to see her smile at his words.

Chapter Three

It was just about noon when we got to my father's gas station. He must have been waiting for us, because the moment we got there he called back to his helper, Owen O'Hara, to look after things and started down the street toward our house. He didn't even seem to notice the bouquet that covered all of Dennis except his feet and his curly black hair. My little brother's chatter about the nice lady and the pizza did not seem to make an impression on him, either. We had to run to keep up with his long, hurried steps.

"Aunt Mabel was just by the garage," he said to me in a low voice so Dennis would not hear. "The baby hasn't come yet."

I felt my stomach do a flip-flop. My poor mother! I began to feel disgust at my father again. He had gotten her into this—the least he might have done was to send her to the Lying-In Hospital! I had heard people say that they had ways in that hospital of making things easier for women. Besides, if there were something really wrong with my mother, there'd be doctors there to care for her.

When we got to the house, I didn't feel like going in. All the way home from the ball field I had been looking forward to Aunt Mabel's frankfurts and beans and brown bread, but as soon as my father opened that door and I heard that first little moan, I lost my appetite. My father hesitated at the foot of the back stairway that led up to the bedrooms.

Aunt Mabel rushed out from the kitchen to meet us. She gushed all over the place when she saw the flowers. Dennis, of course, began shooting off his mouth about the nice lady and her garden. "Maybe the boys ought to take the flowers up to her, Jim," Aunt Mabel said. "It might make her feel better."

He shot her a scolding look and shook his head. "No, I better take them up myself," he said. "I'll tell her you boys brought them for her. Now, you go in and get scrubbed up good before lunch."

I was so relieved that I was not chosen to enter my mother's room that I ran to do his bidding. He was back down before Dennis and I had finished washing. "She loved them," he said in answer to Dennis's questioning, but he did not say another word. He seemed very worried, and this chased my appetite further away. But neither he nor Aunt Mabel nor Aunt Mabel's husband, who came in just as my father came back down, seemed to notice I was not eating.

After a while Uncle Bob said, "Why don't I take Dennis back with me for the afternoon? He can play with my kids. Then Jimmy can go play ball with his friends in peace." Uncle Bob always did understand kids better than anyone I ever knew.

My father nodded. I took an apple and excused myself. The last thing I heard as I went out the door was the muffled voice of Mrs. McGinn upstairs and a strange sound that must have been a gasp from my mother.

I knew I didn't want to go back to the ball game. It would have been nice to sit down by the brook with Ding Coleman or Brian or Aldo and talk a little about what was bothering me, but I didn't want to face the rest of the guys. So I headed for where I always went when I needed peace and quiet: the Sprague House branch library on Armington Avenue.

I loved that old building, with its weather-beaten shingles and its creaking wooden floors always so highly polished, the whole place always giving off a faint, sweet mustiness that made it seem all the more cozy and warm and homey. I was always thankful it had none of the cold marble bigness of the main library downtown. At one time it must have been a fine old homestead, and it still seemed to have all the warmth of a lived-in place.

To enter it, you bounded up three or four resounding wooden steps and into a snug hallway. To the left you found the long, narrow, cozy reference room. It was always fun to work on special assignments here, tracking down information along the rows of encyclopedias and other reference books.

The real treat to me was the circulation room. You had to step down two steps to it. Every time I visited, I paused on that top step and looked about that huge bright room and I was filled with a feeling of adventure and wonder. In the reference room I knew more or less what I expected to find, what I was hunting for, but in this main portion of the library I never could predict what was there waiting for me. It might be the exciting find of some great archeologist in an eerie Egyptian tomb, or the discovery of a South Sea mystic foretelling someone's horrendous fate, or the saga of a white whale, or the uncovering of the fascinating world of microbes.

Most of my friends could never understand that I could find this quiet place so exciting. Neither could my father. "A little more time in the garage and less time in that tomb is what he needs!" he'd tell my mother. Brian Coughlin and Aldo Russo came in quite a bit, but not as much as I did, though. They stuck pretty much to Zane Grey and Fenimore Cooper and did not get into the spirit of searching for new things. They did like to listen to what I found, though, and sometimes would go back and look some of them up themselves.

On that particular Saturday as I stood on the top step and looked toward the circulation desk, I was happy to see that Miss Bessie Worthington was on. She was the young librarian, and she was good-looking, enough so to make even Eats Farrell come to the library once in a while. I guess the best way to describe her is to say she looked like Greta Garbo; at least Eats was always saying that. She liked kids and she helped us a lot in our reference work. If you showed enough interest, she would even help you pick out a good fun book to take home to read. She sure introduced me to a lot of new things!

The place was almost deserted except for a few

adults. I was the only kid in there. Miss Worthington knew more than books. She knew things weren't just right with me right away. "My, I thought you'd be out hitting that old ball today. Anything wrong? You look a little sad," she whispered. In the Sprague House you never talked above a whisper.

I shrugged my shoulders.

"Did you have a fight with your pals?"

I shook my head. How could I tell her what was really bothering me?

"It's none of my business?" She smiled and, of course, I had to smile back.

"That's better," she said. "You don't have to tell me if you don't want to, you know."

But I did want to tell her. I shrugged my shoulders again, then said it right out. "I'm worried about my mother."

It was nice to see sympathy rise up in her soft blue eyes. "Isn't she well, Jimmy?"

I hesitated a moment, felt my face get red, and looked down at the floor. "She's having a baby today," I mumbled.

"Why that's wonderful!" she said cheerfully.

I shook my head. "Mrs. McGinn has been there a long time," I said.

"Who is Mrs. McGinn?" I had forgotten that she was new in Mt. Pleasant. She had come from the downtown library less than a year ago.

"She's the midwife. I wish my father had let my mother go to Lying-In."

"Oh, now," she said, coming around the desk and

putting her hand on my shoulder. "I'm sure she'll be all right. You and your two brothers were born at home, weren't you?"

I nodded, enjoying having her close to me. Eats Farrell would have given his right arm to have her pat him on the head like that.

"There, you see, you're probably imagining too much again. You do have quite an imagination, Jimmy Loughlin!" I shrugged again. "Now go over and choose a good magazine or book and get your mind off things a while."

I walked away from her to the periodical section and picked up a copy of the latest *Boy's Life* and sat down at one of the tables by the window. I soon found I wasn't any more interested in reading than I was in playing baseball. I thumbed through the pages. Here and there a photograph or a cartoon would catch my attention, but not for long. After *Boy's Life,* I tried the *Literary Digest,* then *College Humor,* but not even that could get a snicker out of me.

After a half hour or so I noticed I was the only one in the library, other than Miss Worthington, of course. When I looked toward the circulation desk, her eye caught mine and she rose and walked over to me. "Say," she said, "didn't you tell me you had read about Ichabod Crane in school?" I nodded. "Well, the man who wrote that, Washington Irving, spent a lot of time in Spain, and he wrote about the fabulous Alhambra. Do you know about the Alhambra?" I shook my head. "Well, it's one of the most famous palaces and fortresses in the world. The Moorish rulers of Spain had it built, all tile and mosaic. You do know about the Moors, how they conquered Spain?"

That was news to me, and I admitted my ignorance. She took me by the hand and led me to the History Alcove. There she found me a book. She knew how to hook a guy, all right. For the next two hours I read of the grandeur of the Moors, of their famous warriors, great mathematicians, and rich culture and of how they overran Spain and part of France and settled in Spain.

Miss Worthington got off at four and I left with her, full of questions about the newly discovered Moors. She laughed. "Oh, Jimmy, you probably know more about them than I do now. Tell you what, I'll find you more books on them if you're interested." I told her I was, and then she asked me if I was going right home. I said I thought I'd better wait a while, and she said, "Well, then, how would you like to walk me home?"

I was honored to walk beside her along Academy Avenue toward Atwells, not only because I was proud to have people know she was my friend but also because she was so beautiful. She had her hand on my shoulder and was holding me rather close to her. Roy Oates and Eats Farrell would sure have made something of that! But I wasn't embarrassed enough to pull away from her. I liked being close to her and smelling that delicate perfume she wore and listening to the rustle of her slip against the plaid taffeta skirt and feeling the warmth of her hand on my shoulder.

At Atwells we turned to walk up the hill toward the Polish Catholic church. We turned into a side street after a while, and soon we were standing before a large old house that somehow reminded me of the Sprague House itself.

"You live in this big place?" I said.

She laughed. "Well, yes and no. I don't live in it alone. It's been divided into three apartments. I live on the second floor."

I studied the house. All the shades on the second floor were drawn. I looked at the first floor. Crisp, white lace curtains sparkled at each window. Even on the third floor the windows were bright with curtains. It seemed strange to me that anyone as full of life as Miss Bessie Worthington should not want all this nice bright May sunshine streaming into her house. Somehow those gloomy windows did not seem to fit her at all.

"You like it?" she asked.

I said yes, but, of course, with all those thoughts in my head, I didn't sound too enthusiastic, not until I spied the huge stone chimney running up the side of the house. "Wow!" I said. "Is that a fireplace?" Fireplaces were rare in our neighborhood.

"Yes," she said. "It's a nice-looking old thing, but it's a pain in the neck. I can't use it. The draft is bad. There are leaks around it when it rains. And I think I lose heat up it in the winter. It would be a fire hazard, I guess, if I did try to light it."

"I always wished we had a fireplace," I said.

"Well, you wouldn't want this one," she said.

I shrugged, then asked, "Do you have a big family?"

She smiled sadly. "I live here alone, Jimmy. You see I come from Boston originally. My family is there, my father and mother. I'm an only child." She patted my head. "Be thankful you have brothers, and by now maybe even a new sister. It must be nice."

I suddenly felt very sad for Miss Worthington, alone in this big house. "If you ever need anyone to do errands or anything around the house," I said, "I'd be glad to come over anytime."

"Why that's nice of you, Jimmy! I'll remember that."

I was hoping she'd invite me in right then. I was real curious to find out how she lived. "Is there something I could do now? I've got nothing to do this afternoon."

She answered very quickly. "No, I'm afraid I have to rush right out again. I'm going home to Boston for the weekend."

I'm sure she read the disappointment on my face, because she put her hand on my head again and said, "You ought to go down and play with your friends."

I felt like telling her I'd be happy just sitting in her living room and looking at her fireplace while she got ready to go to Boston. I could even look at her books. It would be fun to see what kind of things she read.

"I'm sorry it has to be this way," she said, "but you see how it is. Where do you play ball, anyway? Someday I'd like to come down and watch you."

I knew what she was doing—trying to get me to think of my friends again so I'd get off her back and go play ball. But I answered her. "At the sandlot at Pleasant Valley Parkway."

When I said this, a look which I couldn't figure out shot to her face.

"It's a nice place," I said. "Have you ever been there?"

She smiled, but I could tell it was forced. "Not

really," she said. "A friend of mine took me for a ride along the the brook there. It's a pretty spot."

"There's not many houses there," I said. "So nobody squawks when we make a lot of noise. There's one nice little cottage close by where we play ball. And, you know, today the lady came out and she talked to my little brother, Dennis, and gave him a piece of pizza and sent a big bouquet of flowers home to my mother."

Suddenly she didn't seem in a hurry to leave for Boston anymore. She asked me what kind of flowers they were. I told her, and then I told her that it was really the first time I had seen the lady who lived in that house close up. "I thought she lived alone," I said. "Maybe she does." But she told me she had a son who used to love to play baseball. I guess he's grown up now."

Miss Worthington grew real curious about that house. "You mean you've never seen any other people go in or out there?" she asked at least three times.

But my own mother used to ask the same question, so I didn't make too much of it and I told her of how sad and lonely that lady looked. I even told her how the lady reminded me of Mona Lisa and how she spoke with a foreign accent and how Aldo Russo had sniffed the pizza all the way over from left field.

Right in the middle of it all she asked the same question, "You mean no one at all ever goes to that house?"

"I've never seen anyone there," I repeated, getting a little tired of it.

"Strange," she said, and started toward the front door so suddenly that it made me feel she just had to get away from me for some reason. She didn't even say good-bye or wish my mother well or anything. I stood there for a while trying to figure it out.

This puzzle bothered me so much that I decided to go back to the ball field. This time I'd really talk to the old lady, I decided. When I got there, I refused to join in the game of Rotation and went to sit by the white picket fence where Dennis had sat this morning.

But now the place really did seem deserted. The lady was nowhere to be seen. I waited a long time. Finally I gave up, deciding that I was making too much of this thing, and I went to join Louie Lennon and Joey Scully from the Fallon Avenue gang in a game of jack-knife under the catalpa tree.

Chapter Four

On Monday afternoon right after school I dropped by the library again. I knew Miss Worthington would be on, and I wanted to tell her about my new baby-sister. Miss Worthington seemed to be expecting me, for she had another book on the Moors on her desk waiting for me. She was very happy to hear my mother had come through everything in fine shape. She even liked the name Agnes, which was my father's mother's name. I wasn't sure I liked it yet; it seemed sort of old-sounding for a pink little thing like my sister.

"It really was a very special day for you Saturday, then," Miss Worthington said, "what with a new sister and Lou Gehrig helping you celebrate by hitting three homers in one game for you." She laughed and she looked prettier than ever. She knew Gehrig was my hero. "I guess it must have been big news down at the sandlot," she continued. "Did you play with your pals yesterday?"

"Just for a little while," I said. "My father was so happy he gave me money to go see Tom Mix at the Castle Theater."

"My, that sister did bring you good luck!" she exclaimed. "Did you take your little brother down to the ball field again?"

"Yeah," I answered, "and, you know, that lady came out again and she gave him some Italian cookies she said she baked just for him, and she sent some more flowers home to my mother."

"She sounds like a fine woman. Did she give you cookies, too?" she asked.

"She told me those cookies were her son's favorite," I said. "It sounds like her son doesn't live with her anymore. I guess maybe he's married or something."

I studied Miss Worthington as I spoke, and I guess she knew it, for she turned her face away from me and stared toward the reference room like she does when one of us is kidding around in there. Only, it was pretty quiet there now. Then just as quickly as she had turned away, she looked at me again and asked. "Did you see anyone else there? Did she have any company?"

"No, she was still alone," I answered. "I kind of felt sorry for her and stayed as long as I could until it came time to go to the show. She wants me to come back and do some errands for her this afternoon."

I thought this last bit of news would bring me a big pat on the back from her, but she said nothing. She checked out the book she had found for me and smiled, an odd sort of smile, like she was pleased and yet hurt, all at the same time. I said good-bye and ran all the way home, wondering what it was about the lady that made Miss Worthington so curious about her.

When I got home, Ding Coleman was already in our yard waiting for me. His name is really George, but we call him Ding because he is so ding-toed that when he runs you'd swear the toes of his left foot, which point in even more than those of his right, will certainly get all tangled up with his right toes and he'll end up flat on his face. The funny part is that he's one of the fastest runners in the gang. I guess the only one who can catch him in a game of Reliev-i-o is Skinny Lanni.

I told Ding to wait a minute while I checked into the house and picked up my brother Dennis. Aunt Mabel was still helping out. My mother was sitting up in the rocker in the kitchen. She must have just finished nursing, because my little sister was snoozing nice and peaceful in her arms. Mother smiled at me. She looked so beautiful it kind of choked me up for a minute.

I had my milk and cookies while Dennis kept telling me to hurry up. He couldn't wait to get to that little cottage again and to get some more flowers for his mother. Bobby, our two-year-old, started to cry because he wanted to tag along, but Aunt Mabel got him quieted down. I was relieved to learn that my mother needed nothing from the store, so a few minutes later Ding and Dennis and I were hurrying toward Pleasant Valley Parkway.

A few of the guys were having batting practice when we got to the ball field. Aldo and Brian hollered to me to get out there and chase a few, but I told them I had an errand to do first and marched across center field to the white cottage. The lady must have seen the three of us coming, for when we got to the back gate, she was already out of the house and she asked us to come in. Ding stayed right with us, for I had told him about her, and he was just nuts about Italian cookies and pizza.

Inside the house, I found myself in a neat pink kitchen. Everything there seemed to be in just the right place. The aroma of tomato sauce was all around us, and it sure made me feel hungry. Ding looked at me, and his big green eyes seemed to grow twice as big and those two dimples of his got deeper as he grinned at me, the same way I'd seen them do while he waited for an ice cream cone to be made up for him at Lappen's.

The lady told us to sit down, then she said, "My name eez Meessus M-m-mo—." She stopped, embarrassed, like she couldn't remember her own name. Then she nodded and said, "Meessus Giordano."

Ding looked at me. I could tell he was a little worried. A woman who couldn't remember her own name? And who lived alone like this? It could be that she wasn't really all there. Did Miss Worthington know this? Was that why she was so curious about her? Was it because she was concerned for my safety?

The lady turned to my little brother. "Meessus Giordano," she repeated slowly. "You can say dat?"

Cocky little Dennis nodded. "Yep. Mrs. Joe Downo!" he said proudly.

Ding snickered, and then we all broke into laughter. The lady laughed, too, and her face lost all its sadness. There was nothing but love in the way she was looking at my brother. I lost all my fears at that moment. It was just her difficulty with the English language that had made it seem she had forgotten her name, I told myself.

"You name?" she asked me.

"Jimmy Loughlin," I said.

She had more trouble trying to say Loughlin than Dennis had saying Giordano, and we all laughed again. When Ding told her that we called him Ding, she really burst out, and then she made a joke about Coleman. "Coal man, you breeng de coal?" And she pinched Ding's cheek. Not many ladies can resist pinching Ding's cheek when he smiles or laughs; the dimples are too much of a temptation.

She turned away from us and bent down to open the oven of the white gas stove. The aroma from the pizza almost brought me out of my chair. It did Dennis. Our eyes popped as she drew it forward and its teasing red surface came into view. But she quickly tucked it in again. "Few more minoots," she said.

She asked me to go the store while we were waiting for it to "feeneesh." All she wanted was a bar of Welcome soap, and she said I could have the coupons from it if my mother was saving them for premiums. I don't think she really needed the soap, because the bar of it I spotted by the kitchen sink was less than half-used.

Dennis was happy to stay behind while Ding and I went to the store. On the way Ding said, "She's a nice lady, but did you notice she started to give us another name, something that began with an M?"

I shrugged. "She just gets all mixed up with her English, I guess," I said.

"She is a little strange, though," Ding said. "Always alone like that. No friends."

"You know," I said, "she really didn't need any soap. She had plenty. I saw it on the sink."

Ding slowed down. "That *is* funny!" he said.

"Maybe we shouldn't have left my brother alone with her," I said, beginning to worry again.

Ding looked at me, and the expression in those big eyes didn't help a bit. I broke into a trot. She was the one who had suggested my brother stay with her. Why had she sent Ding and me off? What if when we got back, both she and Dennis were gone? There'd been a number of stories in the paper lately about children being stolen.

We scooped up the bar of soap at the Nicholson Thackeray store and raced all the way back to the house, not even stopping to answer the questions our friends threw at us as we crossed the ball field.

When we were back in the house, one smile from Mrs. Giordano and all my silly fears were swept away. Dennis was sitting at the kitchen table, his eyes glued upon that huge pizza. She proceeded to cut it into generous strips. Even the crazy notion that she might have been trying to poison us or drug us disappeared. After all, hadn't she given Dennis some pizza on Saturday and cookies on Sunday? Maybe my father was right: I read too much, lived in a make-believe world too much.

Mrs. Giordano gave Ding and me a nickel each for going after the soap. It was more than the soap cost. She even gave Dennis three pennies. Then she sat down at the table with us and watched us eat that delicious pizza. I think she enjoyed it more than we did, even though she didn't have a bite. When we were through, she looked at me and said, "You go play ball now?"

I looked at Ding. He shrugged. She said. "You go. I know you like. Like my son, he crazy for play ball. Dennees an' me, we peeck flor for mamma, nize bouquet."

I nodded and rose. "Your son married?" I asked.

She just stood there without answering for a moment, then a smile came over her face and she said, "My son far away. In Sout' America."

At that moment I felt so sorry for Mrs. Giordano I could hardly swallow, and I had to turn away from her so she could not see me blinking to force back the tears that were trying to come out.

"Let's go play ball," Ding said, starting toward the door. I noticed that his voice was a bit hoarse.

Late that afternoon when we were ready to go home, Mrs. Giordano was waiting for us with another special bouquet for my mother.

Chapter Five

Ding and Dennis and I kept going to see Mrs. Giordano almost every day, and each time she would find some little errand for us to do so that she could give us money. Of course, there were always Italian goodies for us, although the pies she gave us now and then were as good and American-tasting as those my Aunt Mabel made. Twice, my mother and father gave us permission to have lunch with Mrs. Giordano, on Saturday afternoons, and those were really banquets, with luscious spaghetti and meatballs and roasted chicken and potatoes. Mrs. Giordano was a fabulous cook, and a nice lady to be with, too.

Maybe she couldn't speak English very well, but we soon found out she sure knew her baseball. Her son played first base when he was a boy, she told us. He was quite a home run hitter. He could have been another Gehrig if he had stuck to baseball, she said, but he was too interested in automobiles.

She loved to talk about him. I think it helped her forget he was so far away in South America. She told us of how much he loved mechanical toys and of the great things he could do with erector sets. Even before he was ten years old, he could build machines that ran without any help from anyone. Aldo Russo used to join us with her sometimes, and whenever she got stuck for certain words, he would translate Italian into English for her. Funny, Aldo would always blush when he had to speak Italian. I don't know why. I thought it was wonderful to know two languages like that.

By the time school let out that summer and we had organized our Plympton Street baseball team and were ready to take on the Fallons and the Berlin Streeters and the Academies, she had become a real fan of ours. She still would not come out of her yard, but stood there by the white picket fence, watching, usually with Dennis and some of the little kids his age leaning against the other side of the fence, hoping she'd soon produce some surprise sweets for them. On hot days she would make a large pitcher of lemonade for the ball players and she'd have the little guys bring it over to home plate for us, and when we'd look back and wave our thanks to her, her face would really beam.

But there were things that still mystified me about Mrs. Giordano. Ding and I talked about her all the time. Although she herself never seemed to leave the house and no one ever was seen going there except us kids, she still always had a good supply of groceries, and a lot of Italian stuff, too, the kind you had to buy on Federal Hill and could not find in Mt. Pleasant, which was still a mostly Irish neighborhood. And though she spoke of her son in South America and told us he was doing fine, running an auto agency in Buenos Aires, still when summer came and I could keep my eye out for her mailman as he passed the ball field, I never once saw him stop at her home. There was no phone in the house, either. As far as I could see, she was cut off from the world.

The other thing that continued to puzzle me was the interest that Miss Worthington took in Mrs. Giordano. After the day my sister Agnes was born, not once did I go into that library that she did not ask me whether I had visited the little cottage again. She just couldn't hear enough about Mrs. Giordano and kept asking more and more questions and telling me how nice it was of us to be calling on that lonely woman.

It did not take Ding and me long to figure out that someone must be getting those groceries to Mrs. Giordano late at night. We walked past the cottage many evenings just before dark, hoping to see someone going in, but with no luck. Neither of us was allowed to stay out very late, so we knew that to satisfy our curiosity, we would have to sneak out of our homes very late some night after our parents had gone to bed.

It took us about two weeks after we got the idea to get up enough courage to carry out our plans. It was a good thing that we did wait, for in the meantime I studied Mrs. Giordano's grocery situation pretty closely, and soon I was able to observe that on each Wednesday a sudden abundance of food supplies appeared in her kitchen cabinets. This led us to choose a Tuesday night for our stake-out of the Giordano cottage.

It was a terribly hot July night, and this worked against us. I was supposed to meet Ding at eleven o'clock under the Nelson Street bridge, which ran over the brook near the ball field. Whoever got there first was to wait until the other got there and not give up for at least a half hour, in case one of us ran into trouble getting away from home.

It was so hot that night my father put off going to bed way beyond his usual ten-thirty time. I lay upstairs on my bed, listening for him to come up. Everybody else was sound asleep. When he finally did come to bed, it must have been eleven already, and then I heard him begin talking to my mother. "I'll never get away!" I thought. But I began to slip back into my clothes, anyway.

I lay back on the bed, fully clothed, sweating away, picturing Ding under that spooky old bridge all by himself. Now and then I had to sit up to make sure I didn't fall asleep, because to tell the truth my eyes were beginning to feel heavy. After what seemed forever, I finally heard the sound of my father's snoring.

Shoes in hand, I crept out of my room and past my parents'. The stairs creaked like mad as I made my way down, but my father snored on, and I finally found myself outside. I sat on the rear porch and put on my shoes. Then I went flying down Plympton Street.

Soon I realized what a suspicious character I must seem like, racing through the night like that. All I needed was to have the cop on the beat come marching around the corner. I slowed down and began to carefully pick my way down the street, making sure I stayed in the shadows away from the street lights.

When I got to the brook, Ding was already there, but

he was not under the bridge. He was sitting under the lamp post instead. "Are you nuts?" I said angrily. "Come on, let's get behind these bushes! I hope they haven't spotted you already!"

"Gee, Jimmy, it's creepy down there," he said. "I think there's water rats and snakes. I heard them." I could tell he was real scared.

"Where you been, anyway?" he asked. He looked at his wrist. "It's past midnight!" He was wearing Lucky Murphy's watch. Ding's father ran a variety store close to our school, and Ding always had his choice of cowboy and baseball player pitching cards. Lucky's favorite cowboy was Ken Maynard, and Ding had swapped him three Ken Maynard cards for the loan of the watch for a day.

"My father just wouldn't go to sleep," I said. "I hope we haven't missed the delivery."

Thankful that there was no moon out, we shot across Pleasant Valley Parkway. We reached the opposite side just in time to hide behind the giant catalpa tree near home plate before a set of headlights came rounding the bend toward us. I held my breath. This might be it! A moment later the car was past us and Mrs. Giordano's house.

"This is as good a place as any to wait," I said. "We can see both the house and the road." We sat down on the grass at the foot of the tree. I looked toward the cottage. It was all in darkness. "I sure hope we didn't miss it!" I sighed.

Four more cars passed by in pretty rapid succession, each raising our hopes and each scooting right by the cottage. Then there was quite a lull. Ding kept bringing the watch up close to his eyes. There was almost no light at all to read it by. After a while he announced, "It's quarter to one! My old man will kill me if he ever finds out!"

I felt myself getting drowsy. I leaned back against the tree and closed my eyes. Even way back here I could smell the roses from Mrs. Giordano's garden. I listened to the crickets, then to the frogs in the brook. My head was really getting heavy! I shook it to stay awake.

I was getting ready to tell Ding that I thought we should call it quits when the lights of another car popped my eyes wide open again. I felt Ding come to attention beside me.

We both let out a little groan at the same time, as this one, too, sailed right by Mrs. Giordano's. "I'm afraid they've been there," Ding said, and he stood up and yawned.

I was about to follow suit when a strange sound caught my ear, I looked around the tree toward the parkway. I felt my insides freeze, but I tugged at Ding's knickers and whispered, "Get down!"

He dropped beside me. I could feel him shudder as he, too, peered out at what I had spotted.

By the light of the parkway lamps we saw the man approaching. In each arm he carried a bulging, brown grocery bag. I saw what looked like stalks of celery sticking out of one of them. He was a huge man, taller than my father by three or four inches—and my father is a six-footer—and he seemed twice as wide as my father. Even in all the heat, he was fully dressed in a vested business suit, with a white shirt and a dark tie and a soft gray felt hat. When he drew up abreast of us on the road, I could see he had a round, Irish-looking face and he was sweating like mad.

He passed us, and we turned to look after him. He was walking very fast, and in no time at all he was at the cottage. He didn't go to the front door, though. He went along the picket fence that faced our left field and went in the back gate. As soon as he disappeared into her yard, Ding and I, crouching low, raced across the ball field and flung ourselves down on our stomachs by the gate.

We heard the rear door open. We heard Mrs. Giordano's voice say, "Come een!" Come een!" Then we heard the door close. Everything was in darkness.

We waited for the lights to go on in the house, but it didn't happen. We opened the gate and crawled into the yard on all fours. We made our way to Mrs. Giordano's kitchen window. It was open, with the screen in place. We listened, but could hear nothing. Then there was the sound of the shade being pulled down. A moment later we could see slivers of light around its edges, and we knew she had turned on the kitchen light.

Soon we heard her thanking the man and sounding so pleased over this or that item she was removing from the two bags he had brought in. Finally, "Ees so warm!" she said. "I make nize leemonade. You like dreenk?"

He made no bones about being thirsty, and a minute or so later we heard him smacking his lips in appreciation. We'd had enough of Mrs. Giordano's lemonade to know that it's about the nicest tasting you can get anywhere, and, boy, at that moment my mouth sure began to water for some. A sound like a kitchen chair moving over the floor took my mind away from it. The big man said, "I'm sorry, Mrs. Giordano, but tonight I can't stay and chat. I've got another duty to perform."

"I honnerstan'," she said, but she sounded disappointed.

"Is everything all right?" he asked. She must have nodded, for we heard him say, "Good!" Then, "I know you still miss the Hill, but you're better off here. It was the only way, believe me."

"You got no news for me?" she asked.

"No. Things are still the same." The man let out a long sigh. We heard him move a few steps and flattened ourselves closer to the ground in case he was coming out. "There's one more thing, though," he said. "I've seen the way you let those boys come into this house. Do you think that's smart?"

We didn't hear her answer. She probably just shrugged her shoulders. "Well," he said. "I know you must be awfully lonely. I know how you miss your son. And baseball— Well, just don't get too close to them. You know what those kids on the Hill did to you. You don't want that again, and besides— Be careful! Please don't be tempted to go out of this yard. We can't risk you being seen by you know who. I know it's hard, but— You understand, don't you?"

She must have nodded, because he said, "Well, I've

really got to go. I wish I could stay longer. I always enjoy your stories."

"Wait," she said. "I got some rose for your wife."

"You're so thoughtful!" the man said, and he must have thanked her a hundred times as he left, and Ding and I hugged the ground closer.

The light in Mrs. Giordano's went out, and we began to follow the big man across the ball field toward the road, crawling on our bellies most of the way for fear that Mrs. Giordano might be looking out at him. When we got near the corner of Nelson and the parkway, we were able to get up on our two feet again, because it's pretty wooded there.

When the man rounded the corner, we raced in the open to bring him into our sight again. As we poked our heads around the bend, we saw him climb into a car that must have been parked there all the while. The street light close to it shone bright enough so we could tell it was a police car! We watched it drive off, stunned by this discovery.

All the way home Ding and I kept trying to imagine why a policeman, a plainclothesman in this case, would be delivering food to Mrs. Giordano, and in the middle of the night! Nothing we came up with seemed to make sense.

It was a relief to find that my home was still in darkness when I finally stepped in the back door. That little pleasure didn't last for long, however, for I was quickly aware of the rocker in the kitchen making purring noises. My heart in my mouth, I put my foot on that first step that led up to the bedrooms. Then the loud whisper, "Jimmy?"

Thank God it was my mother's voice! She was sitting there rocking by the window with little Agnes to her breast. The hot weather had everybody off schedule.

The first thing I said was, "Please don't tell Dad, Ma! He won't understand!" Then I told her the whole story, except I didn't tell her that the big man had returned to a police car, and I didn't mention the fact that Mrs. Giordano seemed to be hiding from someone.

"He's probably a family friend who works the second shift and can't get there during the day," my mother explained. "She's probably got a heart condition and can't move too far."

I let that go. I didn't want to tell her that Mrs. Giordano worked harder than a lot of men when she worked in her vegetable garden and that she chopped her own wood and scrubbed her own floors.

I didn't get much sleep that night. I had plenty of nightmares. In one of them Mrs. Giordano was a special government agent, and Roy Oates was a big-time bootlegger. Mrs. Giordano was setting a trap for Roy, but I worked for Roy and she was trying to convince me to turn stool-pigeon. Suddenly Eats and Ding and Roy broke in on us, and Mrs. Giordano was shot right through the forehead. She fell into my arms, only, as I looked down at her, she turned into Laura Russo, Aldo's sister, and I began to cry. Aldo rushed in screaming at me, "Look at what you've done to my beautiful sister! And you say you love her!" He came at me with a huge club, and I woke up screaming. My father was standing over me, telling me that everything was all right, that it was just a bad dream.

Chapter Six

It got pretty hot that July, so hot that we spent many an afternoon in the shade of the old catalpa tree just shooting the breeze rather than playing baseball. This, of course, was right up Roy Oates's alley, not only because he was a lousy ball player, but because that summer all that people seemed to be talking about was aviation, and there was nothing in this world more exciting to Roy Oates than airplanes.

Every day in the newspaper and on the radio and on the Pathé News in the movies there was a story of a new air record being broken somewhere. I remember two men kept a plane in the air over Cleveland for over a hundred and fifty hours. Then a week later two other aviators in California topped it by going over two hundred hours. Every country in the world, it seemed, was trying to send a record flight across the Atlantic.

Some afternoons Roy Oates worked at my father's garage, helping with odd jobs. It was the kind of work I'm sure my father wished I could or would do, but mechanical things never did interest me, and I just felt in the way there. But Roy, Roy could bring smiles to my father's eyes with his enthusiasm for machines of any kind. I think he could have taken an entire car apart and put it together again without any help at all from my father.

I must admit it gave me funny little twists of jealousy inside me to hear my father telling my mother about what a "strong, good kid and willing worker and what a mechanical whiz that Oates kid is!" It also made me wonder about how stupid grown-ups can be about sizing up kids. Imagine calling a stinker like Roy Oates a good kid! So I guess it's easy to understand why it bothered me so much whenever I felt Roy leading our bull sessions away from baseball or cowboy movies to aviation.

One afternoon when he and Aldo began to argue about the right location for the Providence airport, I made the mistake of trying to distract him by nodding toward Mrs. Giordano, who happened to be working in the garden. "Boy, that lady sure leads a lonely life!" I said.

The moment I saw Roy's dark brown eyes light up and come to attention, I was sorry I had spoken those words. I had always been very careful not to include him in any of our visits to Mrs. Giordano's house. Oh, he had been over to her fence to say hello and to thank her for the lemonade with all the others after a game, but he had never been in her home like Ding or Aldo or a couple of my other close friends. Somehow, he seemed too rough a character to be near so gentle and kind a lady.

His eyes still on me, he leaned forward, Eats bending toward me with him. "You know, I've been thinking about her lately," he said in a hushed voice, squirming along the grass closer to me. "There's something very strange going on there. Don't you think so, Jimmy?"

I shrugged, feeling my face redden. I began to wonder if by chance he, too, had discovered the secret visits of the man in the police car.

"There must be some reason why she's always alone," he said. "And there must be some reason she's always so good to us. She's hiding something, I bet. She's afraid we'll find it out and tell. If you ask me, I think she's afraid of us."

"And who's asking you?" Eats Farrell scoffed. "Cheez, Oates, you've got a strange mind!"

"Yep," Roy said, paying no attention to his pal and nodding that big head of his, "I think she's afraid of us."

I didn't like the way he sounded, for I knew how much he liked to have people fear him and how he took advantage of that fear. But before I could think about this for long, Roy was at me again with those eyes. "You've been in there a lot." he said to me. "What's in that house? Have you seen any signs of anyone else there?"

I shook my head.

"There, you see!" he said to Eats. "There's something screwy going on there!" He stood up. "Come on, Jimmy! You're her pal. Take me over! We've got to get to know her a little better."

I held back. It was Aldo who made me move. "Let's take him over and get it out of his system, Jimmy," he said to me. "Otherwise, he'll be hounding her all summer."

Aldo and Eats and Roy and Ding and I broke away from the rest of the guys and started toward the cottage, the three big guys in front and Ding and I bringing up the rear. Mrs. Giordano was happy to see us and invited us all into her yard. She had been wheeling a barrow of compost from the far corner to her vegetable garden, and she set it down and walked over to us, smiling. She was sweating pretty heavy and breathing hard.

"You shouldn't be working like that on a hot day like this," Roy said.

Ding and I looked at each other. We were both worried. We knew where this kind of sweetness from Roy could lead. I introduced both Roy and Eats to Mrs. Giordano, and she nodded to them, her smile growing even bigger. Roy said he was very honored to meet her, then rushed over and grabbed the handles of the wheel barrow and asked, "Where do you want this dumped, Mrs. Giordano?"

She went to the garden and pointed to a spot by her tomato plants. Roy took a rake that was close by and asked her if she wanted the stuff spread around. She said yes, and he quickly went to work. When he was through, he asked if he could get more compost for her. She hesitated, but beamed. She really seemed to like him, and it made me wonder again why grown-ups have so much trouble telling a bad kid from a good one.

Roy carried and spread four loads for her while we just stood there like goops. When he was through, she invited us all into the house, which was just what he wanted. She gave us some lemonade and some of those nice, hard almond-flavored Italian cookies. Roy didn't miss a thing in there, those dark, sparkling eyes of his moving and searching around that kitchen every second. Mrs. Giordano loved every minute of it, mistaking his interest for approval of her housekeeping and decorating. Of course, every now and then, he'd stop his munching to tell her how much he liked the flowered curtains and the picture of Rome and the old rocker with the red cushion on which she so happily sat.

When it was time to go, Mrs. Giordano insisted on giving each of us a couple of cookies to take along with us, but when it came to Roy, she went into the kitchen cabinet and took a quarter out of a teacup where she kept her change and handed it to him, "You help me lots," she said. "You come again an' help." His eyes nearly popped out of their sockets.

I was jealous, of course, but then I thought, "Well, that will stop the big lout from thinking she's strange and trying to pry into her secrets."

When we got outside, he turned to Eats and said, "I've got her eating out of the palm of my hand!" He smiled that big-bully smile of his as he looked down at his palm with the shiny quarter in it. "One thing you can be very sure of," he said, "she's going to be very good to us. Yes, she's afraid of us. And she's gonna be more afriad once we find out what's really going on there."

His words filled me with disgust, and even with shame for having been the one who'd led him into her home, but I didn't recognize, even then, the extent of the evil in his threat. It was almost two weeks before the real truth hit me.

It became a habit of Roy's to visit her daily. Each time she would think up some heavy piece of work for him to do, and he would come away with another quarter. I resented this deeply, even though I still ran a few chores for her and got my dime, which I shared with Ding. What really upset me was that she seemed to like Roy so much. Ding and I talked about it every day, and even considered warning Mrs. Giordano that Roy Oates was spying on her. But we decided she wouldn't believe us anyway, he had charmed her so much.

Then it happened. Ding and I were sitting at her kitchen table one afternoon after having gone to the drugstore for aspirin for her. There were plenty of goodies because it was Wednesday, the day after the man in the police car usually delivered groceries to her. In came Eats and Roy. I could tell from the smirk on Roy's fat face when he looked at me that he was up to no good, but Mrs. Giordano, well, she couldn't have seemed happier to see him. He sat down and right away started to peck at the big bunch of fresh grapes in the fruit bowl. He certainly made himself at home there.

After a while he looked up at Mrs. Giordano with a real pushy expression on his face, with what Sister Margaret always called "impertinence." "Mrs. Giordano," he asked, looking her straight in the eye, "who was the man who came here late last night?"

I felt the hair on my neck stiffen, and a chill hit my

spine. I should have expected it! It was easy enough to spot once you got into this house that the food arrived on Tuesday nights. So Roy had posted the place, too! But maybe— Maybe he'd seen some other man.

Mrs. Giordano removed all my hope. I watched her face tense up and her dark eyes grow frightened. It was amazing, though, how quickly she recovered. "Oh, that's a friend of mine," she said, and she really did manage to sound as though she was not disturbed at all. "He does my shopping for me. He brings it every week."

I was glad she had chosen an honest confession. That should stop Roy.

But it didn't. He still had that terrible, victorious grin on his face, and he continued to stare at her until the poor lady had to walk away.

After a while she came back to the table. "You were out verree late las' night," she said to Roy.

"Oh," Roy answered, "my father had to go out of town, and Eats and I went along to keep him company. It was a long drive. I guess it was pretty late when we passed by here and saw your friend with all the bags."

She nodded. That liar, I thought, his father doesn't even have a car!

He and Eats went on picking at the grapes until they were all gone. Then he stood up. "Mrs. Giordano," he said, "could you loan me a quarter until I do more work for you. Eats and I would like to go to a movie tonight."

She nodded, but this time he did not wait for her to go to the cupboard. "That's all right." he said. "I'll get it myself." Even before the words were out of his mouth, his hands were in that cup. I know he took out more than a quarter. I could tell by the jingle in his palm as he proudly swung his fist past me on the way out. "See you tomorrow, Mrs. Giordano," he said, and again he stared right into her eyes until she turned away from him. Only then did he turn and follow Eats out the door.

Mrs. Giordano remained standing by the kitchen sink, frozen, her lips pursed. There was no mistaking the fear in her eyes. After an awkward moment of silence, Ding and I excused ourselves and left, Aldo Russo trailing behind us.

As soon as Aldo had left us and Ding and I were alone, Ding said, "That no-good rat! He stole her money! He's not going to work it off!"

"I know," I said. A strange sadness made my voice break, but anger soon came to clear it. All the way home Ding and I tried to figure out what to do to stop Roy. All winter long after the St. Valentine's Day Massacre, Roy had filled us with stories of the rackets and of how gangsters amassed fortunes by selling "protection" to people in illegal businesses and sometimes even legal ones. We knew only too well how fascinated he was with that terrible idea. Now, did he think he had found a way to sell a bit of protection himself? Poor Mrs. Giordano!

What was it that the lady had to hide, anyway? Certainly it couldn't be anything very bad! Yet why had Roy's threat frightened her so? We wondered if Eats and Roy had followed the man back to the car and discovered it was a police car. If they had, somehow, Roy would have made a point of it. Yet Ding said and I agreed, it was possible that Mrs. Giordano's friend was a detective, but whatever she was hiding from might have nothing at all to do with the law. Maybe she was hiding from a husband who beat her, a drunk, a nut of some kind. It had to be something like that. A bully like Roy could spoil it all for her if he kept sniffing around long enough. Whatever danger she was trying to avoid, he'd sooner or later expose her to it. He thrived on doing things like that.

Ding and I considered discussing the matter with our parents, but we figured that the first thing they would do would be to talk to Roy's parents about it, and everyone knew Mrs. Oates was the biggest gossip in the neighborhood. Once she got wind of the story, everybody would be talking about poor Mrs. Giordano, and in the end all that talk would lead whoever she was trying to avoid right to her.

That night as I lay in bed, I could think of nothing but how I had ruined Mrs. Giordano's security, and the guilty feeling made me sick to my stomach. I thought of a dozen plans for stopping Roy, but all of them seemed to end the same way, in some action that would only make things worse.

I thought of Miss Worthington. Now there was someone who'd want to help. She always seemed so interested in Mrs. Giordano, but in the end I knew if I told her about the man in the police car and about Roy, she'd go to Roy's folks, too, and we'd be right back where we started again. Besides, there was something strange about Miss Worthington, too. After that first time that I walked her home from the library, I planned things so that I'd be at the library at closing time quite often. I must have walked her home six or seven times after that. Each time I said things to let her know I'd like to be invited into her house. I'd say, "I'd love to see that stone fireplace," or, "I bet you get a beautiful view of downtown from your windows." But she never did let me in. Once I even ran an errand for her, got some cold cream from the drugstore, but when I got back to the house, she was waiting outside by the gate for me. It was very strange.

The only conclusion Ding and I could make the next day was that we had to know more about Mrs. Giordano's secret before we could act. We decided that on the next Tuesday night we'd listen again by her kitchen window. Maybe this time the man in the police car would stay longer and they'd talk. We hoped Roy Oates and Eats had not made the same plans.

Chapter Seven

Even baseball couldn't keep my mind off what was happening at Mrs. Giordano's during those six slow-poke days before Tuesday. Every afternoon, after each game, Roy would barge right into her house without any invitation at all. Eats would go right along with him. I was surprised at Eats, because usually he is a nice, easygoing kind of guy, but I guess he just had to show Roy he had guts or something. Ding and I always made sure we followed right behind them. If we were going to help Mrs. Giordano, we had to know everything that was going on.

After the second day, Roy did not even bother to ask Mrs. Giordano if he could borrow a quarter. He would just strut over to the teacup and help himself to some change. He never did any more work for her, either, but just kept saying: "I'll stop by one of these days and help you weed."

Poor Mrs. Giordano just stood there, not knowing what to do. I could tell from her eyes that she was angry with him, but she said nothing. Once I saw a tear come to her eye as she sadly turned away from him, shaking her head slowly. Right then I almost told Roy what a louse I thought he was, but I couldn't get up quite enough courage.

Ding and I agreed that for Roy to be acting as boldly as he was, he must have found out a lot more than we had been able to when we had listened by the kitchen window. "He's probably threatened her with whatever he knows when we weren't around," I said.

"Maybe we ought to ask Roy straight out," Ding said.

"No," I said. "It won't do any good. Roy likes secrets too much. But Eats—Eats likes to show how much he knows. Maybe we can get something out of him."

So it was that we approached Eats one night while we were all hanging around the corner street light and Roy was lording it over all the little guys, telling them all about the movies he had seen lately. And he had seen plenty, with all the money he had been stealing from Mrs. Giordano! We took Eats aside and found him more than willing to talk.

"The cops are watching her," he said. "We found out that much. The other night we saw a couple of other men watching the house, too."

"Was one of them the man who brings the groceries?" I asked.

"Oh, no," Eats said. "These were different guys. But I think they were cops, too. She's part of something pretty bad for cops to be watching her like that, I tell you!"

"But why would they be bringing her food if they think she's bad?" I asked.

"From what we could hear listening under her window when the man with the groceries came," Eats said, "she used to live on Federal Hill with her brother. I guess she's a widow. Well, the kids down there got on her for something that happened and almost drove her nuts. I guess it was this cop that got her out of there and hid her in the house down by the ball field."

"It doesn't make sense," Ding said. "Why doesn't her brother come to see her or to live with her?"

"Because the cops don't want her talking to anyone!" Eats said with his know-it-all air. "I don't think even her brother knows where the cops hid her. They just don't want her talking to anyone." His eyes lit up with excitement. "Roy and I figure she knows too much. Some gang will have her killed if they find her."

The thought gave me a chill, but I still found it hard to associate Mrs. Giordano with anything evil. It made me angry to hear Eats so positive about it. "They could have killed her while she was still on Federal Hill if that was true," I said. "It doesn't add up to me."

Eats shrugged. "Well, that's all we could hear. There's a lot more we gotta learn, but we will!"

"Why?" I asked. "So you can blackmail her?"

"That's what you know about it!" Eats sneered, putting on his superior airs again. "What we're doing is gonna help the cops. She knows plenty she's not telling them. What Roy's doing is trying to break her down. One of these days we're gonna lead the cops to just what they're looking for. And we'll be heroes, Roy and I!"

"Aw, bunk!" I said. "He's just stealing money from a poor, frightened woman."

"Stealing from crooks isn't stealing!" Eats said.

"Mrs. Giordano's not a crook," I said. "And you know it! I notice you don't take any of her money."

"No," Ding said, "but he lets Roy pay his way into the show and buy him ice cream and stuff with it."

"We're not stealing," Eats said, his voice getting weak. He walked away from us. He had a hurt look on his face, and I knew this had been troubling him all along.

Ding and I decided to go for a walk around the block. It was just beginning to get dark, but there was a bright moon out and a nice cool breeze. There were quite a few people strolling up and down Academy Avenue, happy that the hot old sun had finally gone in. We didn't say much, and when we got to the junction of Academy and Chalkstone, we just stood there for a while watching the trolleys rounding the corner and the crowds filing in and out of Lappen's ice cream store.

Suddenly I spotted a familiar figure moving down Academy toward us. It was Miss Worthington, looking very beautiful in a white linen dress I'd never seen on her before. When she saw me, she came right to us. She was not alone. There was an older woman by her side.

"Well, isn't this nice," she said. "Mrs. True, I'd like you to meet one of my best customers at the library,

Master James Loughlin and this is his friend, George Coleman—Ding, they call him. Ding's starting to read quite a bit himself lately."

I blushed.

"Boys," Miss Worthington said, "we're going to Lappen's for ice cream. I'd like to treat you both, too."

I felt a little embarrassed and was ready to back away from her offer, but Ding's eyes told her how much he liked ice cream, and so she laughed, and we fell in beside them and walked to Lappen's.

On the way out, I thanked Miss Worthington and then said, "I saw Mrs. Giordano today."

To my surprise, she did not ask me how the lady was, as she usually did. Instead, she turned to me and asked, "And how's that Plympton Street baseball team coming?"

I thought this very strange and tried once more to bring up Mrs. Giordano. I wanted her to keep the poor lady fresh in mind, for I was sure that one of these days I'd be going to her to ask what I should do about the Roy situation.

"We just practiced today," I said. "Tomorrow we're playing the Fallons." Then, "Mrs. Giordano brought us lemonade again today," I added.

She didn't even seem to hear what I had said. "Well," she said, "I guess you boys want to run along and not follow a couple of fuddy-duddies. See you soon, I hope."

I felt pretty bad about Miss Worthington losing interest in Mrs. Giordano like that, so bad I hardly tasted the flavor of the orange-pineapple as Ding and I made our way back to the corner of Chalkstone and Academy, munching on our cones. "Say, why don't we take a walk down by the brook," I said. "Maybe Mrs. Giordano will be sitting in her garden."

"Funny," Ding said, "I was thinking the same thing."

We made our way up Academy to Justice Street, where we turned in and headed toward Pleasant Valley Parkway. When we got to the point where Justice, Nelson, and the Parkway meet and the brook takes a sharp turn to run along Nelson, I felt Ding's hand on my arm. "Look!" he whispered.

On the other side of the brook, facing up Nelson, a big, black automobile was parked. From the parkway lights we could see there was someone sitting at the wheel. The driver must have heard us approach, for he turned, then catching sight of us, started up the car and, without putting on the headlights, drove off up Nelson past Mrs. Giordano's. There was enough light for us to catch sight of a bald head and a pair of very broad shoulders. We also saw that there was another, taller man sitting next to the driver.

"They were watching her house!" Ding whispered, as though out of breath.

"They must be the two cops Eats was telling us about," I said.

"They don't look like cops to me," Ding said.

"I know," I said. "Let's go under the bridge and wait a while. Maybe they'll be back."

"I can't wait long," Ding said. "It's late. My father'll scalp me when I get home."

"Just a few more minutes," I said. We raced down

the bank of the brook to the underside of the bridge.

We waited in the dark, listening, watching for headlights. Each time a passing car lit up the road, we climbed out of the tunnel and up the grassy bank on our stomachs. We did this four times and were just about to give up when we heard another car approaching, much more slowly than any of the others. Up went our heads. There were no lights on on this car. It rolled around the corner onto Nelson and stopped. Through the rear windshield we could see the moon light up the same bald head.

"It's them!" Ding whispered, altogether too loudly.

We watched for a long time, but nothing happened. The car just sat there. Ding became more and more worried about getting home late, and after a while I, too, began to worry about facing my father's anger.

We decided to give up and come back the next night. We crawled back down the bank, took off our sneakers, waded across the brook and crept up the other side. We even stayed on all fours as we crossed the other side of the parkway. Once we got to Canton Street, we broke into a trot and raced for home.

We were crossing Chalkstone when Ding looked back and panted, "They're following us!"

I turned, but in the glaring headlights behind me all cars would have seemed the same. I thought I did see a shiny head, though, but I couldn't be sure, not at the speed I was running, nor was I going to slow down to check. I put my head down and made straight for home, getting up all the speed I possibly could. When Ding branched off at his house, I didn't even turn my head.

Chapter Eight

That shiny bald head kept coming back to me all that night, in crazy, mixed-up dreams that always made me end up sitting up in bed in a cold sweat. Even while I was awake it stayed with me, and the face that went with it kept changing in ugliness a hundred times a minute, always scowling and threatening. I tried to get my mind off it by watching my little brother, Dennis, sleeping so peacefully in the bed next to mine, but the questions kept whirring around in my head.

Had that car really followed Ding and me home? But why would they be after us? Was it because of something Roy and Eats had done? But Roy and Eats had said those two were cops—did they really know that? Maybe they weren't! Maybe they weren't even the same two that they had seen! Those men, particularly that bald-headed one, didn't look like cops!

The next morning when I went down to breakfast, I felt very tired. My mother asked me if I was sick. I forced myself to brighten up and eat some oatmeal for fear my father would tell her I needed castor oil. After he had left for his garage, I came very near to telling her about what had been happening at Mrs. Giordano's. The way things were going, sooner or later I'd have to get some grown-up's help, that was sure. But I was still afraid she'd run right over to Roy's mother, and that lady would certainly make things worse for Mrs. Giordano.

I didn't play very good ball against the Fallons that day, and that afternoon, right in the middle of the game, I told my team-mates I had an errand to do and left to go to the library. Earlier, from center field I had watched Roy and Eats go into Mrs. Giordano's, and I knew I had better be doing something before things went too far in that cottage. Miss Worthington would respect my secret if I asked her to. She'd advise me what was best to do.

I got to the library a half hour before closing time, but my heart sank when I saw the white-haired Mrs. Anthony behind the check-out desk. Where was Miss Worthington? I looked into the reference room behind me. The place was empty. Then I remembered, and I grew angry at myself. This was the Saturday Miss Worthington had off.

I went to the magazine section and poked around with *College Humor* and *Judge* for a while, not really looking at anything, playing with the idea of going to Miss Worthington's house. It still bothered me that she had never once invited me into the place. But I finally realized I had to do *something.* I shrugged and started out of the library.

As I stepped up to the level on which the reference room is located, I froze. There, with his back to me, standing by the encyclopedias, was a short, broad-shouldered, bald-headed man! That head! That could be it! Was he still following me? The man turned. I held my breath. I saw his face. It was not ugly at all, just sort of pale and plump and kind of ordinary.

I told myself there were thousands of bald heads in this city and started to breathe again, but I cleared out of that library in a hurry, without ever looking back, and ran all the way to Atwells Avenue and up the hill and around the corner to where Miss Worthington lived.

When I got to the house, I couldn't make up my mind whether to ring the front doorbell or go up the back stairway to the second floor where she lived. I stood there looking up at her windows, wondering why all her shades were pulled down and the windows closed. On a hot day like that you'd think she'd be trying to pick up a bit of breeze. Suddenly I heard someone call to me. "Oh, hello there, Jimmy!"

I went to the side of the house where the sound seemed to be coming from. There at a first-floor window was the lady who had been with Miss Worthington the night she'd bought Ding and me ice cream at Lappen's. I was surprised she remembered my name. It took me a while to remember hers. Mrs. True, it was.

"Looking for Bessie?" she said.

'Bessie?" I asked.

"Miss Worthington to you, I guess," she laughed.

"Is she home?" I was beginning to lose my nerve and to hope her neighbor would tell me she was out.

"Oh, she's up there. Probably reading away. I tried to get her to go for a walk earlier. It's such a beautiful day! You go ahead up! She'll be glad to see you. It'll do her good to get her face out of those books and her ears out of that radio for a while."

I nodded, and since I was already in the side yard, on the walk leading to the rear door, I decided to go in that way. As I went in from the bright sunlight, the darkness of the black hallway blinded me. I had to feel my way to that first step, but though I could not see, I certainly could hear, for Miss Worthington's radio was on full blast. I followed the sound to the second floor landing. There I waited for my eyes to clear, but now my mind began to get hazy. Whatever in the world would I say to Miss Worthington?

My first knock must have been a bit weak, for I still had half a mind to turn and go back down those stairs. But I knocked again, louder. I waited, but there was no answer. The music from that radio was much too loud. Maybe she was taking a bath, I thought, and she had the volume high so she could hear it from her bathroom. I knocked again, harder still. No answer. Well, if she was really in the bathroom, it would take her a while to get ready to come to the door.

I waited a long while. Then I really pounded on the door and pounded again. Still no answer. Could Mrs. True have been wrong? Could Miss Worthington have gone out without her seeing it? But then the radio wouldn't be on, would it?

I put my ear against the door, listening for sounds other than those from the radio, but that music would have drowned out a cannon going off in that apartment. I banged the door again and rattled the knob. Then I began to worry. Could something have happened to Miss Worthington? Was she ill? Alone in there, unable to move? Worse, a beautiful lady like that, alone—some nut could have broken in and—I decided to go downstairs and tell Mrs. True about it.

I was halfway down the stairs, when I heard the doorknob above me turn. I looked up and there stood Miss Worthington staring down at me. She didn't give me her usual big smile. I guess she was too surprised to see me. I had guessed wrong about her being in the bathtub, because she was all dressed up and looked pretty warm, her face covered with sweat.

I backed up the stairs. Her face finally did break into a smile, but it was a sort of timid one and it gave me a strange feeling, like maybe she wasn't happy to see me, not at that moment at least. But she did ask, "Were you going away?"

I didn't want to admit I was worried about her, so I just said, "I thought there was nobody home."

She put her hand on my shoulder and let me into her apartment. "I guess with this music I didn't hear you," she said. "You'll have to learn to knock louder."

"What and knock the door down!" I felt like saying, but I didn't say anything and began looking about her kitchen. It was probably the cleanest and neatest I've ever seen. Pale yellow walls and nice flowered hangings at the window and a little table covered with a tablecloth that matched the curtains.

"This is a nice surprise," she said.

"I wanted to talk to you about Mrs. Giordano," I said. "Funny things are going on, and—"

She steered me out of the kitchen into her living room. I noticed that the shades that were drawn when I first looked up at her windows were now raised and the room was nice and bright. It had pale green walls and a maroon divan and stuffed armchairs and bookcases loaded with books and a big super-heterodyne console radio which was still blaring away. But the real gem was the gigantic stone fireplace. I'd never seen one so big in all my life! Of course, this was no ordinary tenement house. It was an old mill owner's mansion that had been done over.

She turned off the radio. The quiet sure sounded good! We sat down on the divan facing the hearth, and I just couldn't keep my eyes off all that beautiful stone, almost the whole wall of that room, except for the windows to the right of the fireplace.

"Boy, I'd have a fire in there every day!" I said.

She laughed. "Not on a hot day like this, I hope!"

I was embarrassed by the foolishness of my words. She saw it and tried to make me feel better. "I know what you mean," she said. "I guess in its day it brought a lot of cheer to the people who lived here."

I wanted to say that it was nice to look at even without a fire and that it would even look nicer if she had some logs sitting there, although I bet those logs would have had to be as long as my father is tall to reach across those old andirons. I got up and walked over to touch the shiny brass lion heads on the andirons.

Suddenly Miss Worthington seemed to become very

impatient. "I thought you came to talk about Mrs. Giordano," she said.

I returned to the divan. I had to search for the words for a few seconds, but once I had started, I found it easy to tell her about the man in the police car who brought the groceries to Mrs. Giordano every Tuesday. This did not seem to surprise her as much as I thought it would. She said it was probably a family friend who worked for the police department, just like my mother had, and just like my mother, she said that Mrs. Giordano was probably too weak to do her own shopping. When I mentioned that Mrs. Giordano worked like a horse in her garden, she asked me to tell her more about what Ding and I had heard by the open kitchen window that night. She liked the part where Mrs. Giordano gave the man some roses for his wife. "She seems to be such a lovely lady!" she said.

For a while after that neither of us spoke. I sat there in front of the great stone fireplace and listened to the loud ticking of the clock on the rugged wooden mantel, trying to decide how I would tell her about Roy Oates. She knew Roy. She had helped him find books on auto mechanics and on aviation many times. She didn't know what a bully he was.

Miss Worthington put her hand on my knee. "Jimmy," she said, and looking up into those beautiful blue eyes of hers, I could see she was really worried, "Jimmy, who else besides you and Ding know about this man in the police car?"

"Too many," I said, and I knew I'd have no trouble now telling her of Roy.

She pulled her hand away from me. When I told her that Roy and Eats knew and that Roy was using the information to get money from Mrs. Giordano, she shot up out of her seat. "How awful! How awful!" she kept saying, pacing up and down across the hearth. "I can't imagine anyone being that mean!"

"I know," I said. "I wish I was bigger. I'd show that Roy!"

She came to sit beside me again. "No," she said, "you musn't antagonize him more! We've got to think this out. Don't do anything for now! I'll let you know what I decide, and then—"

She rose as though to dismiss me. I never thought such a calm person as Miss Worthington could ever become so disturbed. She seemed so upset I almost decided not to tell about the bald-headed man, but then I realized that was the real reason I had come here. "That isn't all, Miss Worthington," I said, and I told her of the two men who had been watching Mrs. Giordano's house. She had become very pale, and it seemed to me her hands were trembling. But I had to tell her everything, else how could she advise me?

"Roy and Eats saw those men, too," I said. "They think they're cops. Why would cops be watching Mrs. Giordano? You don't think she's done anything wrong, do you, Miss Worthington?"

"Oh, no, Jimmy," she said, putting her hand on my head and pulling me toward her until my face touched her shoulder. Would Eats and Roy have loved to have seen that! It did feel good, though, and she smelled so nice!

"Was he a big man, the bald-headed one?" she asked.

I shrugged. "He was sitting in a car. It was dark. He had big shoulders. I'm sure of that." I hesitated, then, "I think I saw him again."

She straightened up. "When?"

"Today. In the library."

I heard her suck in her breath. Then she sprang to her feet. The fear in her eyes frightened me at first, but after a while the idea that she cared for my safety so much made me feel good.

"You saw him in the library?" She didn't seem to want to believe it.

I nodded. "I can't be absolutely sure it was him," I said. "I guess every bald man looks suspicious to me now."

"How big was this one?"

"He was short, but rugged."

"I don't like it! I don't like it!" she said in a panic and began to pace around the room. "I don't like the idea of people following you, Jimmy!"

Again she came over to me and pulled me close to her, and again I really enjoyed feeling her next to me like that. "Jimmy," she said, "we've got to keep very quiet about all this until I figure things out a bit. Don't even tell your friend, Ding, about the man in the library! By tomorrow, you and I will decide what to do about all this."

I nodded, amazed at how troubled she was. I would have liked to have talked to her more, to tell her that she was exaggerating the danger she thought I was in, but she was already on her way to showing me out.

"You run all the way home as fast as you can, Jimmy, so no one can follow you," she said.

The way she said these last words really did scare me. Did she know something I didn't know about all this?

I ran out of her yard up toward Atwells as fast as my legs could move. By the time I got to the church at the corner, I was completely out of breath, and I stopped.

I was panting away, my head almost down between my knees, when I felt a shadow fall over me. I looked up. My heart stopped. I felt all my strength leave me, and I had to lean against the iron churchyard fence.

It was the bald-headed man who had been in the library! He had crossed over from the opposite side of the street.

"You sure can run fast, kid!" he said. I was surprised at how soft and even pleasant his voice sounded.

A little of my fear left me, and I forced myself to look squarely up at him. "I mustn't let him know how scared I am," I told myself. "Besides, he may really be a policeman like Eats said, that is, if he's the same man that Eats and Roy saw. But if he isn't, if he's another guy, someone evil, up to something bad, then I better stall for time until I get my breath back, then through the churchyard and over a few back fences. He'll never be able to catch me. He's too fat for fences!"

"I was just starting down the street here when I saw you come barreling out of the Worthington house," the man said.

"Liar!" I felt like crying out. "You've been following me all day, and God knows how long before that. And how do you know it was Worthington I was visiting? There are two other families in that tenement." But of course, I said nothing.

"Do you run errands for her all the time?" he asked. His face became creased with a smile, but it was a smile that brought panic back to me. Never before had I seen a smile make a person ugly. This one wrinkled up the man's entire face and curled his lips up like a dog baring his teeth so that he seemed to change into a snarling monster. I gripped the iron fence tightly.

"You see, I run a tobacco store," he said. "Her husband left his wallet in my store."

His normal expression returned to his face, and I was able to answer, "She has no husband."

He broke into a hearty laugh, and although this did make him look ugly, it was nowhere near as frightening as his smile. "Ho, ho, that's right! They told me at the library it was *Miss* Worthington. It must have been her brother then."

"She has no brother," I said. It made me feel good to contradict him.

Suddenly, that terrifying smile was back on his face. "Heh, heh, it must be a boy friend she's keeping up there."

"She lives alone!" I said angrily, hurt that anyone could think that of Miss Worthington.

"You sure, kid?"

"Yes, I'm sure!" I answered hotly.

He shook his head. "That's funny," he said, disappointed.

Then he asked again, "You run her errands for her?"

"Yes." I lied. "I'm in and out of there all the time. She lives alone."

He shrugged. "I guess the wallet belongs to somebody else," he said. "See you around, kid." He left.

I watched him until he disappeared down the avenue. Then I started for home, my legs feeling a little wobbly under me now.

Chapter Nine

I was almost halfway home before I realized that the information I had given the bald-headed man had put Miss Worthington in a very dangerous spot. I had told him she lived alone. That was probably all he had wanted to find out from me. This thought not only made me very angry with myself for being so stupid, but it worried me so much that I turned right around and started back to warn her.

This time, however, I took a different route. I took the nearest hill that runs from Academy to Mt. Pleasant, looking carefully along each street I crossed, checking every car that passed me and stopping now and then to look behind me. At every hedge, at every big tree, I expected that bald head to come popping out at me. When I got to the top of the hill, I turned and headed toward Olneyville Square, following one of the streets that runs parallel to Miss Worthington's. I went way beyond where she lived, then doubled back, approaching her house from the opposite direction I had the first time.

When I got there, the coast seemed clear. I glanced up at her windows. All the shades were drawn again. I wondered if this had something to do with the bald man and also why he should be watching both Mrs. Giordano and Miss Worthington, although I still couldn't be absolutely sure it was the same bald head in each case.

As I started up the back stairway, I heard her radio blasting away again. Just as it had happened the first time, I knocked and knocked on her door without getting an answer, but this time I had the bald-headed man to worry about. Had he already been here and done harm to her? Was he still in there? In a panic I began to rattle the doorknob, then run to the edge of the stairs, ready to plunge down them in case it should be he who opened the door. I did this several times, my mind picturing her lying in front of the fireplace, strangled or with her head bashed in. Each time I came nearer and nearer to rushing out of that spooky place.

When, finally, I saw the knob begin to turn, I really got the shakes! Who would appear? Would it be the man with the evil smile? I stood at the edge of the top step, ready to leap down if I had to.

The door swung open. I could feel my shoulders sag in relief. It was Miss Worthington. She did not seem pleased to see me. She was still dressed the same, but she was sweating more. She stood there as though she was not going to ask me in.

"What is it, Jimmy?" she asked, sounding impatient.

"I-I-I-I've got to talk to you," I said, looking back down the stairs. "Alone."

She nodded and let me in. She led me through the kitchen and into the living room, and I noticed that the shades were up and the windows open and the radio shut off. I sat down on the divan in front of the fireplace, and she stood there before me, looking very puzzled, not seeming to know what to say.

"Miss Worthington," I said, "you remember I was telling you about the bald man in the library? Well, when I left here a little while ago, he was waiting for me down the street, at the corner of Atwells. He must have followed me from the library."

I watched her clench her fists, and when I looked up into her face, I could see the color leaving it. Her eyes became as frightened as mine must have been when that man first approached me at the corner. Her whole body went stiff as an electric light pole. I thought she was going to pass out, so I stopped talking.

After a while, she said in a very soft voice, "What did he say to you?"

I told her exactly what he had asked and what I had answered. I thought she'd faint for sure as she moved forward and plopped down onto the divan beside me.

"I guess I shouldn't have told him you lived alone," I said.

She turned and looked at me as though she was seeing me through a fog, then shaking her head slowly, she said, "No, Jimmy, you did the right thing."

It took her a while to get hold of herself, but when she did, she patted my head. "You handled yourself well," she said, "better than most grown-ups could have." Then she asked me to go over the whole thing again, describe the man, repeat his questions. Suddenly she got up and, nodding her head, began to pace up and down, up and down in front of the fireplace, wringing her hands.

"Who is he, Miss Worthington?" I asked.

This brought her back. She came over to me and took both my hands in hers. "Jimmy," she said, her eyes staring right into mine, "we've got to keep this to ourselves. Just for a while. Promise you won't tell anyone! Not even your parents. And, Jimmy, you better not come here anymore, at least not for a while, not until I tell you."

I nodded and she squeezed my hands. "Good boy!" she said. But as we started toward the kitchen, she grabbed me by the shoulder and pulled me back. "No, that won't do!" she said, excited all over again. "You've already told him you run errands for me. We've got to make things seem normal. No, you must come every afternoon for a while, and I'll send you out to the store." Again I nodded.

As I was going out the back door, I just had to ask her, "Miss Worthington, are you in trouble?"

She tried to laugh in the way grown-ups do when kids trap them with a question. "Oh, no he's just a pest who'd like to date me," she said. But her laugh didn't fool me. I was looking right into her eyes and she was plenty scared.

When I got home, supper was already half over, and I thought my father, who was very strict about our being on time for meals, would surely send me up to bed without supper. This would have been bad, not because I was hungry, but because on the way home I had stopped at Ding's and we had planned to go down to the parkway and look for the bald-headed man again tonight. I know I had promised Miss Worthington not to tell anyone, but Ding and I always shared our secrets. Besides, I had to tell someone, just in case that bald-headed guy was really somebody bad and came after me and kidnapped me or something.

My father was angry at me, all right, but he allowed me to sit at the table and my mother to serve me the lamb stew. After a while, he asked me where I'd been. When I told him I'd been at the library, his face got red. Then he said, "On a nice day like this, he coops himself up in that dusty old place! Growing boys need air and sun and exercise, Margaret!"

"He played baseball all morning and part of the afternoon, Jim," my mother said. If she had said nothing at all, I think he would have dropped it at that, but Mother has to always defend me, and he doesn't like that at all.

"You don't learn from books!" Father said. "You learn from doing! That Roy Oates, it makes me feel so good to watch the way he works at the garage. He knows nearly as much as I do about automobiles. And he's always eager to learn more! A fine lad!"

I thought, "If I ever tried to tell him Roy Oates was a bully, that he was stealing from an old woman, why he'd slap me across the face and tell me to stop being jealous!"

Of course, I *was* jealous. Imagine, my own father

thinking more of Roy Oates than he did of me! But now was no time to argue. I couldn't risk being confined to the house tonight. I had to find out if the bald-headed man who was spying on Mrs. Giordano was the same one who had followed me.

After supper I helped my mother clear the table and do the dishes. I was in no hurry to get out. Ding and I didn't want to get to the brook until dark, anyway, and we didn't want to get into the game of "Kick the Can" the gang would be playing at the corner, because if things went as they usually did, Ding would end up being "it" for the rest of the night. He was absolutely the world's worst in this game.

Instead of going out, then, I helped my two brothers put together a little bridge with our erector set. This pleased my father, because on my own I had added a couple of extra spans to the bridge described in the directions. "That's beautiful, Jimmy!" he said. "See that! You really can work with your hands when you want to!" I was sure happy then that I had chosen to do this instead of going up to my room to read the book about the archeologists in Egypt that Miss Worthington had picked out for me. When I said I was going out for a while, my father had completely forgotten he was angry at me.

It was still not quite dark when I whistled for Ding at his house. We jumped his back fence and then the Smiths' and got out to Chalkstone Avenue without any of the gang seeing us. We decided to walk down to Davis Park and back to use up time until it got dark.

Chapter Ten

There was no moon out that night, and Ding and I felt pretty brave as we made our way toward the ball field, running from tree to tree along the brook in the dark. When we reached the street lights of Nelson Street, however, it didn't take long for our courage to desert us. I think that right then if either of us had said, "Let's go back home!" we'd have both done an about-face on the spot, because parked right in front of Mrs. Giordano's cottage was the car that had followed us home last night!

We decided to make a run for the big catalpa tree by home plate. "Hey," Ding said as we stepped into the safety of its darkness, "there's nobody in that car!"

We snuggled up against the trunk of the tree, both our heads swiveling around to search the area. It was a long time before either of us spoke again. Then Ding said, "Maybe they're both in Mrs. Giordano's."

I noticed that the pitcher's mound was in complete darkness and that the rays from the street light didn't quite make it past the third base line onto the field. I plopped down on my belly and whispered, "Come on!" We started to crawl out toward the mound.

When we got there, we stopped and listened. "Stay low!" I said as the beams from the headlights of a car rounding the corner almost reached us. Out there in left field Mrs. Giordano's house seemed a million miles away. Her kitchen light was on. "I wonder if they're really in there with her," I said. We started crawling across the infield toward the house.

We stopped quite a few times, not only to catch our breaths because if we got to panting too loud someone might hear us, but also to do some listening of our own. Old baldy might be here in the night with us, waiting to see who was coming to call on Mrs. Giordano. Maybe he had parked the car in the front of the house to make us believe he was inside. Maybe it was a trap. Maybe he wanted us right out here, and he was waiting for us behind the gate or by the big tree to the right of the gate. Maybe it wasn't Mrs. Giordano at all he was interested in. Maybe it was just me—me and Miss Worthington.

I kept feeding myself courage by thinking that, perhaps, there really were two different bald men and that this one was a policeman, just as Eats had said.

"The window's open," Ding said when we drew close to the gate.

"Sh-sh-sh!" I warned. We lay still for a few seconds. I thought I could hear voices coming from the house.

"You hear something?" I asked.

"Yeah. They're in there talking to her," Ding said.

I shushed him again. Then I reached up, still lying

down, and unlatched the gate. The squeal of the hinge made me freeze.

"Who's that?" It was a deep, hoarse whisper, and I knew it was not Ding's voice. My wrists snapped from the chill that ran up my spine and down my arms. So he *was* out here with us!

I flattened myself hard against the ground, feeling Ding pressing close beside me. His breath seemed very noisy. I wanted to tell him to stop breathing, but I didn't dare to open my mouth. After a while I looked up. I saw a shadow move in the light that was coming from the kitchen window. "I thought I heard something," someone said.

That voice—I knew that voice! But out here everything seemed so strange and scary, it was hard to tell what was real and what was not. Was I just imagining? Had I really heard it before?

Then another voice. "Get down!" it commanded. "You're gonna screw up everything!"

"It's Roy and Eats!" Ding whispered.

I gave him a shot in the ribs with my elbow to shut him up, but it was too late. Two shadows moved toward us.

"Get down!" I heard Roy order again. I started to crawl backward on my stomach, but found that the gate had closed behind us. I changed direction and headed toward Mrs. Giordano's flower garden, Ding right beside me. Too late. The kitchen light caught just enough of us, and Roy and Eats were down on us like cats on a couple of mice.

When they had us pinned down, Roy whispered,

"Cripes! It's Jimmy and Ding!" He was all out of breath. He puffed a while, his weight on my chest so that I could hardly breathe myself. "All right," he said finally, "you two guys made us miss enough already. Now crawl back to the window with us—and not a sound!"

The four of us made our way back to the open window and lay under it, flat on our stomachs. A deep, gruff voice reached us. "I searched the whole yard, Early. There's no one out there."

"That's him! That's him!" Roy whispered, all excited. "Early Winters! I knew she had something to do with gangsters!"

"Wow!" Eats said.

But the news that the state's foremost gangster was in that house didn't really sink into my mind at that moment, for I was too busy listening to poor Mrs. Giordano crying her heart out. Another voice was saying to her, "Now, please, don't cry! We're only trying to help you and your boy."

This time I had no trouble recognizing the voice. It was one I could never forget. It belonged to the man who had followed me from the library. So that was Early Winters, the man everyone feared! How many times had Roy Oates played his tough-guy part in our gangster games and roughed me up! And now—this was for real! Why had Early Winters been following *me*? I shuddered and listened, my heart beating so hard I wondered if they could hear it inside the house.

"My boy—he dead!" Mrs. Giordano sobbed.

"Oh, no, no, no!" Early Winters insisted, almost

gently. "You mustn't say that! That's what the police want us to believe. We think he was just shot in the arm, probably just a scratch. He couldn't die from that. They just don't want us to find him. They don't want us to help him. They want to force him to come to you so they can arrest him and charge him with murder."

"My boy no keell nobodee!" Mrs. Giordano moaned. "He jus' drive."

"Unfortunately, he's the only one who lived to say that, and they'd never believe him!"

The poor lady's sobs grew louder.

"If you really love your son," Early said, "you'll tell us where he is, Mrs. Montella."

Roy Oates sprang to his knees as though shot in the rear with a BB gun. "You hear that?" he whispered, altogether too loudly. "Mrs. Montella! She's Evo Montella's mother!"

"Wow!" Eats Farrell said again, this time forgetting to keep his voice low.

"What was that?" the voice of Early Winters called out. It had lost all the softness he had been using on Mrs. Giordano. Its harshness made my hair stand on end.

We hugged the earth and held our breaths. But even in my fear, my heart went out to poor Mrs. Giordano. I just couldn't believe the son of such a kind lady could ever be a killer. I thought of the stories she told us of how he loved to play baseball and how he loved to teach the little kids to play. That part of her story must have been true, I felt sure.

I remembered how almost a year ago the newspapers had been full of stories about the great three-way gun battle that happened when G-men came upon some hijackers in the process of attacking a bootlegger's truck. A young man named Evo Montella had been driving the truck. The two men with him had been killed. He was never found. Everyone said he had been driving for the Early Winters gang, but no one had ever been able to connect Early with it. The two G-men had also been shot dead. My father had been so amazed to discover that this Evo was the same young man who used to come to his garage for automobile spare parts. He was an artist with a motor, my father used to say, but his undoing was that he loved cars too much, particularly fast ones.

Things were strangely quiet in Mrs. Giordano's, or Montella's. I was thinking of lifting my head again when I thought I heard a footstep. I looked up, and there against the light from the kitchen window I saw the huge shadow standing over us. I tensed my muscles, rising to my knees just a bit, ready to spring out and then over the picket fence behind us. I felt my insides shiver and said a quick prayer. I dared to look once more before I moved. It was the man who'd been in the car with Early last night. I could tell from that huge head and that wild mass of hair. It was the same silhouette.

The man lunged at us. "Why you—"

The four of us were up on our feet together. Ding and I made it to the fence first. Eats was right behind us and caught up with us on the other side.

We turned to look for Roy. He had never made it out of the light of the window. The big man had an armhold on him and had Roy's arm right up to the middle of his back. Roy began to holler, "Ow! Ow!" at the top of his lungs.

"Oh, cheez," Eats said, "we gotta help Roy!" He had hardly taken a step when who appeared by Roy's side, taking his other arm, but Early Winters himself, his bald dome glistening in the light.

The three of us watched the two men march Roy quickly toward their car. "Oh, no!" Eats cried out. "They're gonna take him for a ride! They'll rub him out for sure! He knows too much! What'll we do?"

I was surprised to find out that as much as I disliked Roy Oates, I still considered him one of us, and I wanted no harm to come to him, not like that, anyhow. It was almost like the feeling I sometimes had for my little brothers when they were being regular pests, but would do something dangerous like run out in front of an automobile. It would scare me half to death and make me realize how much I really did care for them.

"We gotta help him." I said.

"But how?" Eats said, and he sounded as if he was going to cry.

"We'll throw stones and make a lot of noise," I said, "Maybe it'll scare them off."

I remembered that when we had cleared the ball field this spring, we had piled up a lot of rocks just outside third base. I started toward that spot, and Eats and Ding knew at once where I was headed. "Let him go!" I started to yell. "You lousy gangsters, let him go!"

Ding and Eats joined me. "We're calling the cops! Let him go!" they called out.

The three of us began to throw stones. I heard a couple of them hit the car. "Let him go! Let him go!" we kept screaming.

"Hey!" Early's voice rang out. "Stop that! We just wanna talk to him a minute. Then we'll give him back to you."

We watched them take Roy into the front seat between them. Eats really began to cry now. "We shouldn't have let them do it," he sniffled. "It's a trick! Now we can't stop them! They'll just drive off with him!"

I tried to tell him it wasn't so, that big gangsters wouldn't risk getting into trouble over kids. Then we all quieted down for a while, and a funny thing happened to me. I began to forget about Roy and to think about Miss Worthington. I thought of the closed windows and the drawn shades and the loud music and of how long it took her to answer the door and of all the questions Early Winters had asked me about a man in her house. A terrible question kept popping up in my mind. Could it be that she—?

Eats was tugging at my sleeve, sobbing again. "We've got to do something, Jimmy. Let's run for the phone in the yellow house on the other side of the brook and call the police."

"If they were going to take him away, they wouldn't be sitting there like that," I said.

This quieted him down again. We sat and waited. My mind returned to Miss Worthington's apartment. She could easily have been hiding a man there. And all that interest in Mrs. Giordano—

The car door swung open. Out stepped Mr. Early

Winters' henchman, that head of his looking bigger than ever. Then came Roy. The two of them shook hands. Then Roy ran toward us as fast as all that weight of his would let him.

When he reached us, we were all surprised to find he did not seem scared at all. "C'mon!" he said, sounding like his old self and starting toward the catalpa tree, where it was good and dark. We sat down at the foot of it and watched Early Winters' car drive away. Suddenly Roy reached over and grabbed me by the shoulder, so hard I had to cry "Ouch!"

"Jimmy, you got me in a helluva jam and you're gonna get me out!" he said, letting go.

"What happened?" Eats asked.

"This little punk here," Roy said, giving me a sharp jab in the ribs, "has been carrying messages between Evo Montella's girl friend and his mother. Early wants to know where Evo is, or he's going to have my hide!" He leaned over and put his fat fist right under my chin. "Do you understand that, Loughlin? You're gonna tell me everything or I'm dead! And I'm telling you, before I go—" He grabbed me by the shirt and gave me a shove that sent me flying on my back.

"I don't know what you're talking about," I said, sitting up again.

"Don't give me that crap, Loughlin! Early told me all about following you to Miss Worthington's house. He's been watching you for a long time running between her and Mrs. Giordano."

"Miss Worthington doesn't even know Mrs. Giordano," I said. "I still don't know what you're talking about."

"Don't cross me, Loughlin! I'm in big trouble with Early Winters and so are you! It didn't take him long to find Mrs. Montella when the police moved her from Federal Hill to here and changed her name to Giordano, and it didn't take him long to find out that Evo's girl worked in the Sprague House library. He's been watching them both for months. You're the first connection between the two, and he says you see them both almost every day. So don't give me that stuff! You know she's hiding Evo!"

"I've been all through her house," I lied, realizing that all I'd ever seen of Miss Worthington's apartment was the kitchen and living room. "There's no man there. That Early's dreaming. He's got the wrong girl."

"Oh, no!" Roy said. "He's got the right girl, all right! He's been up there a few times. He's searched the place. Maybe Evo's not staying with her, but she's hiding him somewhere. Early says you're always running errands for her and that you know more than you're saying. Well, I'm gonna help you run those errands, and you're gonna help me find that Evo, or I'm gonna cave your head in, you understand?"

The thought of Early Winters searching through Miss Worthington's apartment made me angry. "Listen, Roy," I said, spitefully, "I'd tell the police before I'd tell you or that lousy Early Winters!"

Now he really jumped on me and began to swing away at me like a madman as I fell back on the grass. In the dark I could not see to guard myself against his punches. I tried to roll away from him, but all his weight was on me. I felt his fist hit the side of my head, then my right eye. I guess this was the closest I'd ever come to being knocked out. For a second or so I didn't really know where I was, until I heard Eats saying, "C'mon now, Roy, take it easy!" and felt Roy's heavy body being lifted off me.

I lay there for a while, listening to Roy panting and wondering whether I should roll away in the darkness and then run for home. But I was too curious. I wanted to know more about what Early Winters had said about Miss Worthington and Mrs. Giordano, or Montella. What if it were all true? What if she was really hiding him in her home? It was possible. But all this time? It was nearly a year since that shoot-out. Had he been there all the time? Had they been living as husband and wife? And poor Mrs. Giordano, she really still thought he might be dead or out of the country. She'd said it to that policeman and to Early, too.

My thoughts were interrupted by the sound of sobbing. I sat up in amazement. It was Roy Oates, crying like a baby! It was the first time I'd ever heard him break down like that. Eats was patting him on the back, trying to quiet him down.

"What's the matter?" I whispered to Ding, who was squatting next to me.

It was Roy himself who answered, still sobbing. "They'll kill me if I don't find out for them! They know he's alive, they said. If the cops find him first, they'll kill me!"

No one said anything for a while. It made me feel

bad to see Roy so frightened. I guess I should have been as scared myself, but my mind was still not wanting to believe that Miss Worthington could ever be part of anything bad, and I kept telling myself this was all a mistake and that sooner or later Early Winters would realize it.

Eats came over and put his arm around me. He was always the big politician in our gang. "Jimmy, you're not going to let a friend down, are you?" he said. "We've always stuck together, haven't we? And we're in this together this time, too, aren't we, pal?"

I pulled away from him. "I wouldn't let anybody down," I said. "But I don't know anything! That Early guy is just imagining I do!"

"You lying bastard!" Roy hollered through his sobs. Once more I felt his weight come crashing down upon me. This time I was fast enough to slip out of his reach and up onto my feet. Out toward the parkway I ran, making for home, thanking God that Roy Oates was as big and clumsy as he was.

"I'll get you, Loughlin!" I heard him calling after me. "You're not bagging me! I'll get you!"

Chapter Eleven

My mother let out a screech when I stepped into the kitchen that night. I didn't realize until then that my right eye was nearly closed from Roy's punch. She rushed over to look at it closely. "What happened?" she asked.

I kept my good eye on my father, who sat in the rocker in the corner reading the *Evening Bulletin* and listening to the radio. First, I'd been late for supper and, now, this! "Somebody hit me with his knee when we were playing King of the Mountain," I lied.

He looked up from the paper. I trembled to think what he would do to me if he caught me in a lie To my surprise, a big grin broke over his face when he caught sight of my shiner. "That's a beaut!" he said. I should have known! He always liked it when he thought I had been playing rough.

"Oh, this is terrible!" my mother kept saying.

"Margaret, please stop fussing!" he said. "He'll get many of those before he grows up. It's good for him. Toughens him up." He winked at me. I tried to smile back, but I really felt bad about lying to them. Besides, I had a lot to worry about.

I got very little sleep that night, and what I did get was loaded with nightmares. Each of them ended with a sort of St. Valentine's Day Massacre, usually with all of our gang lined up against Aldo Russo's chicken coop wall and with a bunch of bald-headed men, all looking like Early Winters, coming at us with machine guns firing away.

After each nightmare I tried to stay awake by planning, but my thoughts kept fighting each other. The right thing, I kept telling myself, was to tell my parents everything. But then, I thought, my father would want to go to the police, and poor Miss Worthington would be in trouble. I probably should go to her first, give her a chance to convince her boyfriend to give himself up. Then she wouldn't be involved. If it is true that he was just driving the truck and didn't do any shooting, and if he would help the police by testifying that the men who shot the G-men belonged to Early Winters' gang, then things wouldn't be so bad for him. But Early Winters wouldn't stand still for that! He was out to kill Evo, because Evo was the only one who could testify against him. Even if the police could protect Evo after he was found, Early would go after Miss Worthington and Mrs. Giordano. He'd get even somehow.

No matter how I figured it, Miss Worthington was in danger and so was Mrs. Giordano and so was I and, yes, so was Roy Oates. Roy had every right in the world to be scared and to want to beat my brains out. After all, I did get him into this mess. But what a strange situation! I really didn't know if Miss Worthington was hiding Evo, and I really hadn't been carrying messages between the two women. And, yet, who would believe me, even if I were to swear on a stack of Bibles a mile high? Probably only my mother.

And so it went all that night, my mind whizzing back and forth without coming up with any idea that made sense. I was still trying to lose my confusion when I heard my father getting up in the next room. It was Sunday, and he liked to go to seven o'clock Mass. I usually went to the children's Mass at nine o'clock. Roy Oates generally went to nine, too. So I decided to go to early Mass with my father. Even if Roy was out early, laying for me, he wouldn't dare lay a hand on me with my father around. He'd never do anything that might make my father stop him from coming to work on cars at the garage.

My father laughed again when he saw my black eye that morning, and he said it was all right for me to go to seven o'clock with him because he understood how I felt about having the nuns and some of the girls at the nine o'clock see me with such a lulu of a shiner. Even on the way to church when some of his friends stopped to say hello and joked about my eye, he seemed to enjoy the attention and to be proud of me. I wondered what he would have said if he had known Roy Oates had done it. Probably something like, "That Roy does fine work!" I bet.

After church as we turned into our street, I spotted Roy Oates waiting by our gate. The minute he saw that my father was with me, he took off in the opposite direction. I felt my heart begin to pound. Roy would never let up on me. Somehow, I had to get this thing settled and soon! It wasn't just the thought of the beatings he'd give me that worried me, but the idea that his life and mine were truly in danger and, even worse, the fact that, even though I hadn't meant to, I had caused all this trouble.

I didn't eat much breakfast, and my mother kept asking me if it had something to do with the black eye and if I had a headache, while my father kept telling her not to baby me.

Afterward, being careful that no one noticed, I went from window to window in the house, looking for Roy outside. I finally caught sight of him from the front window in the living room, standing across the street, leaning against McDonough's fence, his eyes glued on our front door. I went to the back door, slipped out, jumped over the rail of our veranda, then over our neighbor's fence, and scooted across their yard and over the next fence to Chalkstone Avenue. I was on my way to Miss Worthington's.

It was a very hot day, and I was covered with sweat when I got there. Again I noticed that all her front windows were closed and the shades drawn. As I started around toward the rear door, the glider under the maple tree in the back yard caught my eye. Miss Worthington and the lady downstairs were swinging gently back and forth in it. They stopped their swaying when they saw me.

"What happened to you?" Miss Worthington asked, rushing toward me, all worried.

I remembered my black eye and I began to blush and I lied again, "I got bumped playing King of the Mountain."

Mrs. True started to laugh. "A mighty funny-looking king!" she said.

Miss Worthington didn't seem to think it was humorous, "You look pretty warm," she said. "Why don't you sit down here with Mrs. True a minute, and I'll go up and fix us all a lemonade."

"Oh, I'm going in, dearie," Mrs. True said. "I've got to get the Sunday dinner started."

The two women started toward the house, and I began to follow. Miss Worthington turned to me and said, "I'll be right down, Jimmy. Wait for me on the glider. We can talk there."

It was obvious she didn't want me in that house. Why? Was she really hiding Evo Montella there? I went back to the glider and sat down.

A moment later I heard the windows on the second floor being opened and the blaring of a radio pouring out of them. I looked up. My mind was see-sawing again. Roy had said Early Winters hadn't been able to find a trace of Evo up there. Maybe it was all a crazy mistake, just like it was with me. Early was convinced I was carrying messages between Miss Worthington and Mrs. Giordano, but I wasn't even sure the ladies knew one another. Maybe Early had the wrong girl friend. Maybe it was some other librarian, maybe one from downtown or some other branch.

But then what was all this business of opening and closing windows and blasting away with a radio? She must have been covering up something up there. Yet, she was hardly the type who would take up with a gangster. But maybe Evo wasn't a gangster. My father had said he never thought Evo was the kind of young man who would be mixed up in the rackets, that the only thing wrong with him was that he loved fast cars too much.

When Miss Worthington came down, she was carrying two nice tall glasses of cold lemonade. I drank mine down in almost one long gulp. As I was emptying my glass, I could see she was studying me with a very worried expression. "Now," she said as she took the glass away from me, "what really happened?"

I hesitated, searching the yard with my eyes. You could never tell when Early and his henchmen or even Roy Oates would be sneaking up on us.

"You'd rather tell me upstairs?" she asked.

I nodded, and with her glass still unsipped, she led me back inside. Upstairs, she opened the door with a key, let me into her kitchen and started to lead me toward the living room once more. But this time I was determined to see more of this apartment. "Miss Worthington, may I use your bathroom?" I asked.

I thought this would give her a start, but she simply nodded and showed me into the hallway behind the kitchen that led to the bedrooms. I found the bathroom as neat and sparkling as the kitchen, all pink and white and feminine and delicate. I guess it was just what I would have expected in the home of a beautiful and gracious lady like Miss Worthington. I looked behind the shower curtain. I opened the medicine cabinet. No sign of masculine things. This place was all girl!

When I came out, she was not in the hallway, so I quickly peeked into the bedroom across the way. It must have been her room, all white and frilly with Cape Cod curtains and an eyelet spread. I even dared to raise the coverlet and look under her bed. No sign of anyone there, no men's shoes or socks or anything like that.

I didn't quite have the guts to go to the next room, reserving this for another trip to the bathroom. I returned to the kitchen. She was not there, but when she heard my footsteps, she called me into the living room. I found her sitting on the divan. All the shades were up and the windows open, and a cool breeze was blowing across the room. I sat down beside her.

"Now tell me what happened, Jimmy," she said.

I thought it was about time we both laid our cards on the table. "Miss Worthington," I said, "I know Early Winters has been here."

I watched her straighten up and draw a deep breath. It was a while before before she answered, and it was with another question. "And how did you know that?"

I told her about what had happened last night at Mrs. Giordano's with Early and his henchman and Roy Oates. She grew paler and more nervous at each bit of information I gave her, and just as she had done the last time I was in that room, she ended up pacing back and forth in front of the fireplace. While I was waiting for her to say something, for some crazy reason I began to think about the fireplace and of what Christmas cheer the light from the burning logs must have spread. That was a fireplace just made for Santa Claus, I thought. And then the idea hit me!

"Miss Worthington," I said, "I feel funny. I think I need a drink of water."

This brought her out of her fog. "What's wrong?" she asked, bending over me and touching my forehead. "You *do* feel warm."

"I guess I've been sweating too much," I said. "I need a drink."

She went off toward the kitchen. I shot to my feet and went straight to the hearth of the fireplace. I hesitated, looking toward the kitchen to make sure she was out of sight, then stooped down and looked up the chimney. I did not look far. My throat tightened and I held my breath. There, swaying a few inches above me, were the soles of two shoes! I pulled back in terror. Yes, I'd seen the cuffs of trousers, too! There was a man dangling there! Maybe a body! The thought pushed me back.

But I had to know! I shivered and slid forward again on my knees. Slowly, I poked my head under once more. My eyes peered around the masonry. It was dark, but the flue must have been open and there was just enough light. Yes, it was a man, all right! Sitting in a sort of swing! I couldn't see his head. His knees and his lap were in the way. Thank God for that, for it meant he couldn't see *me*. He was alive, all right! I could tell from the way his legs were moving.

I rushed back to the divan and waited for Miss Worthington. All my insides began to tremble. God, if he should ever come down out of that swing—He was part of Early's gang, wasn't he? He'd murder me, all right! I thought of getting up and running out of there, but that would only be telling them that I knew.

Miss Worthington came back into the room. "You do look pale, Jimmy," she said. "Here, drink this. It's nice and cool." She felt my forehead again and smoothed back my hair.

I began to sip on my lemonade. A nice lady like this would never be hiding a murderer, I thought. It must have been the way my father said. Evo was just a driver. The police wanted him so they could get the Winters gang for the murder of the G-men. Winters wanted him dead so he couldn't testify. It was Winters he was hiding from, not the police. The poor guy, a year cooped up in here! Climbing into that swing in the fireplace each time someone came to the door! The radio going full blast so no one could hear that there was someone in the house besides her!

When I finally set the glass down, she said, "I still think we need to keep all this quiet just a bit longer, Jimmy. I know you'd like to tell your parents, but we're both caught in the middle of something we don't understand. I don't know any Mrs. Montella nor any Evo. I've got to have time to convince Mr. Winters that he's made a mistake with me and with you."

Her words made me angry. Here she was, asking me to help her by keeping quiet, really asking me to be her partner, so why wasn't she telling me the truth? I felt so hurt by the thought that she did not trust me that I almost said it: "Miss Worthington, why are you lying to me?" But I remembered the man in the fireplace. Of course! She'd have to check with him first before she could let me in on their secret.

I rose. "Miss Worthington," I said, "I better be going. My parents will be looking for me."

She followed me to the door. She squeezed my shoulder. "Jimmy, you'll keep our secret, now, won't you?"

I nodded and ran down the stairs.

Chapter Twelve

I took the shortest route home from Miss Worthington's, running all the way, thankful that the streets were still filled with people going to and coming from Mass. I didn't look either to the left or right for fear some friend might stop me to talk and slow me down. The secret I was carrying was much too frightening!

Miss Worthington had made me promise to be quiet about this thing a bit longer, but just how long would I be able to keep such terrifying information inside me? Real soon I would just have to tell someone. My mother, probably. I'd need help, for sure! Early Winters wouldn't wait. He'd be after Roy again and Miss Worthington and then me! And, now, with what I knew, would I be able to keep lying and covering up? If I slipped just a bit, it would be good-bye for Evo and even for Miss Worthington maybe, and for Roy and Ding and me and probably poor old Mrs. Giordano! I thought of the St. Valentine's Day Massacre, with all of us lined up against a cement wall waiting to be mowed down. I began to feel sick.

My father's gasoline station was open until noon on Sundays. When I reached it, I did not slow down even then, for I thought Roy Oates might be hanging around there. I waved to my father who was pumping gas and kept right on running. Knowing that my mother was alone at home, I made up my mind as I rounded the corner that I would tell her what had been happening to me.

I expected to see Roy waiting for me in front of the house again, but it was Ding who was sitting on our back steps. His clothes were all mussed up, and his eyes were red, as though he had been crying.

"What's up?" I asked.

"Roy," he pouted, "I think he's gone crazy. He thinks you've been telling me things. He gave me an awful sock in the stomach. I still feel sick. I never saw him so mad. Even Eats won't go with him today."

"Where did he go?"

"Where else? Down to Mrs. Giordano's. He's gonna get her to talk, he says."

"But she doesn't know anything," I said. I knew my words sounded too strong, and I caught Ding staring at me as though ready to ask, "Why, do *you*?" That secret was sure trying to get out of me. I just had to be more careful!

"Roy's scared," Ding said. "He's liable to do anything."

"We better go down and try to calm him down," I said.

"Are you nuts?" Ding said, rubbing his belly.

"But we can't let him push that poor lady around. She's been so nice to us," I said.

Ding didn't move. When I was halfway down the street, I heard him come chasing after me. When we got to the ball field, we found Aldo Russo was already trying to get a game of Rotation going. His sister, Laura, and a couple of her girl friends had come down to watch. She always looked so beautiful in her Sunday dress!

Aldo was calling to us before we even got close to the field. "Hurry up, you guys! We need you to get started!" How I would have loved to go out there and hit a few long balls for Laura to see! But I wasn't going to let her see me today, not with this shiner of mine! I kept walking straight along the road past them, putting my hands in front of my face so they hid my eyes and shouting back, "Can't. Gotta run an errand for Mrs. Giordano!"

Of course, Ding kidded me. "What's the matter? Afraid to let your girl see you looking so pretty?" I walked faster.

When we got to the back door of the cottage, I knew we had arrived none too soon. Through the screen I could hear Mrs. Giordano sobbing, "I know notting!"

Roy's voice sounded very angry. "Now, lady, you're only gonna get us both in trouble if you don't tell me!" he said.

I felt the blood rush to my head. "Leave her alone!" I shouted as I burst into the house.

Mrs. Giordano was sitting at the kitchen table, her

head in her hands, her shoulders heaving away as she cried. Roy was standing over her, his face red. His eyes really did look crazy as he whirled around to face me. He rushed up and grabbed me by the shirt. I could hear Ding gasp behind me. "Now, you gonna tell me where he's hiding?" Roy's voice trembled as he shook me.

I've got to admit I was scared. He pushed me back across the room, knocking over a couple of chairs, and pinned me against the wall.

"Don't, Roy! Don't!" Ding cried out. Mrs. Giordano started to scream.

Roy held me with one powerful arm and with the other got ready to punch me. I moved. Not quite in time. A glancing blow caught the side of my head. It felt as though my ear was being ripped away. I let out a howl of pain and fear as my hand went up to feel if my ear was still there.

"Leave him alone!" Ding shouted. I could see Roy getting set for another swing at me. "Leave him alone or I'll go get his father!"

The expected punch didn't come. I looked down at my fingers and saw the blood from my ear. When I looked up again, Roy was backing away, and a strange change was coming over him. As he looked at my bloody fingers, his eyes seemed to lose their madness and become worried.

Ding kept repeating, "I'll go get his father if you don't leave him alone!" Mrs. Giordano was whimpering, but now she had a broom in her hand and began to bring its handle down on Roy's back. Roy was too rugged to feel her blows, but he continued to back away from me. There was no doubt now about the look in his eyes. He *was* worried! What was it?

Suddenly, it hit me. Of course! Who was the one person in all this world he would not want to cross? My father! He would never risk losing my father's good will. It meant too much to him! That garage, that freedom to work on automobiles, the opportunity to learn more and more about motors—all this meant more than anything else in the world to him!

With this thought, I suddenly felt well-armed against the bully. "Listen, Roy," I said, "you better lay off this poor lady! I'm warning you!" I was amazed at the firmness I was able to bring to my voice. "If you ever want to work with my father again, I'm warning you, you'd better lay off! If he ever knew— "

"Knew what? Knew what?" Suddenly Roy was threatening me with his fists again. But this time I wasn't scared. This time I looked right into those dark brown eyes and I could see how troubled they were and that he was coming after me only to cover his own fears.

"If he ever knew you were helping a gangster like Early Winters," I said calmly, "he'd never let you into his garage again."

Roy stepped away from me and stood there in the middle of the kitchen for a while, pouting. Then, looking down at his feet, he said, "Your father would understand."

"Like hell he would!" I said. "My father's a very

honest man. When I tell him how you've been stealing money from this poor lady and how you want to help those crooks—"

"I really wasn't stealing money," he said, his eyes still on the floor. "It was just a game. Ask Eats. I gave most of it away."

Mrs. Giordano returned to the table and began to sob again, softly.

"But it was her money," I said. "No, Roy, boy, I'm afraid you wouldn't want my father to know that!"

He looked up and walked over to me as though he was getting ready to take another poke at me, but he didn't. I could see his anger returning, though, and I walked away from him and took out my handkerchief and began to wipe away the blood that was trickling down my neck. My ear was now throbbing like mad. "Boy!" he said. "Can't you dumb clucks understand? We're in trouble! This lady is the mother of a gangster! He's part of Early's gang and Early wants him. If we don't help Early, he's gonna let us have it, all of us!"

"Roy, believe me," I said, "there's nobody here that can help him. Mrs. Giordano doesn't know where her son is. Miss Worthington doesn't even know *who* he is. I got caught in the middle because I happen to go to the library and to come here. That Early's got it all wrong! He's adding up two and two and getting fourteen! He's trying to get information out of us that just isn't there."

Roy walked away from me. "He doesn't seem to think so," he said. "Maybe you're telling the truth, but I don't know about this old lady and that librarian."

"You tell 'em, Roy!" a man's voice sounded out.

I froze, stiffer than any statue. No one had to tell me whose voice that was. The screen door slammed, and in walked Early Winters' henchman. I gulped. Had he been listening at the door all the while? Even Roy was petrified when he saw the big man walk in. Only Mrs. Giordano didn't seem to be afraid. She stood up, drew a deep breath to stop her sniveling, then pointed to the door and said in as loud a voice as I've ever heard her use, "You, go! Dees, my house! You, go!"

But Early's sidekick acted as though he didn't even hear her. He went over to Roy and said, "You're doing all right, kid. Now, give us just a little more help and you'll be off the hook. You gotta hold these people here until I go find out what Early wants to do about what I heard here."

Roy was too scared to answer. Mrs. Giordano let out a scream, then began to hit the gangster across the back with her broomstick. This seemed to make the man half-crazy. He reached into his coat pocket and pulled out a gun. "All right!" he barked. "Enough!"

He backed the four of us, Roy included, against the wall. All I could think of was the Valentine's Day Massacre and the terrible dreams I had had last night. I felt my knees knocking and Ding trembling against me. Early Winters would have handled this differently. But this man— This man was a wild man! This man could lose control! This man could kill!

"Not you," he said to Roy, and he motioned him to step forward. "You've gotta help me."

Roy obeyed, but I could see he was as frightened as any of us as he took his place beside the gunman.

"Now," the man said, "no one gets hurt if you do what I say. Roy, you open that cellar door and we'll all go down there."

Panic took me. Why was he taking us downstairs? Was this it? Was this the execution that had been haunting my dreams? Maybe we shouldn't be letting him lead us like a flock of frightened sheep. Maybe it would be smarter to make a run for it, *now*.

But that gun seemed so close! I allowed myself to be herded into the cellar with the others. The place was neat and clean like the rest of Mrs. Giordano's house, but that long, gray back wall made me shudder. The gunman lined us up against it, just like in that dream. Roy stood pale and trembling by his side. Mrs. Giordano reached into her apron pocket, drew out her rosary beads, and began to pray.

"Now you hold them here until I come back!" the big man ordered Roy. "And you know what happens if there's any monkey business! You understand?"

Roy gulped and nodded. The man handed him the gun. "Here, you'll need this. I won't be long. And, kid, don't screw up, or else!"

He bounded up the cellar steps, and Roy stood facing us alone. He was afraid of that gun, I could see that. He was afraid to put his finger anywhere near the trigger. The revolver just sort of dangled from his hand. Where was the tough, rough bully who'd forced us into the chicken coop so many times this spring, prodding us firmly with his toy gun?

"You're not going to do it, are you, Roy?" I asked

after a while. "We're your friends, not them. You're not one of them."

"Shut up!" he hollered, but his voice only told me how full of terror he really was.

"You know right well if we decided to run out of here, you couldn't shoot us," I said. "That dummy should have known better than to leave us with you. Early will kill him when he finds out what a dumb thing he did." I took a step forward, "So come on, let's go, Roy!"

"Get back there!" he screamed. I saw his hand tighten on the gun. Maybe he was scared enough of them to do it, I thought, and stepped back to the wall. On one side of me I could hear Mrs. Giordano praying in Italian, on the other, poor Ding letting out one long sigh after the other.

"Look," Roy said a few seconds later, "why can't you guys see that this is the best way? They'll let us go afterwards. Why get them mad?" He was almost pleading with us to go along with him.

"We could go right now," I said. "Why wait?"

"They'd kill me!" he said.

"I never thought you'd be such a yellow belly," I said, my eyes on the gun, which was now dangling loosely again in his hand. "They're after me as much as they're after you. Sure, I'm scared, but I'm willing to take a chance to do what's right." I could see my words were making him feel bad, so I kept right on talking. "I don't know how you could want to be on the same side as rats like that. And when I think of how much my father thinks of you! Roy, how do you think he'd feel if he knew that right now you were holding a gun on his son? And for Early Winters? Boy, you could forget ever working in his garage again, that's for sure! You'd be lucky if he ever even looked at you again!"

The hand that held the gun dropped to his side. "You wouldn't tell him, Jimmy, would you?" He seemed about to cry.

I knew I had him, "What do you think?" I teased.

His shoulders sagged. Now was the time, I thought. I had tackled him before in our football games, big as he was. Maybe once out of five times I'd been able to put him down on his back. I rushed him, staying real low. This time I hit him at the knees, just right, and down he went. The gun went flying across the room. In a second Ding was on top of him, punching away, and then Mrs. Giordano moved in with the handle of a garden rake. But Roy was putting up no resistance. He just lay there, and in a minute we stopped hitting him.

"Can't you see," he sobbed, "I wanna be with you guys?"

"Then, let's go!" I said. I took Mrs. Giordano's hand and started up the stairs. "You two guys head for your houses and don't come out for the rest of the day!" I yelled back down to them.

"Jimmy," Roy called after me, "you're not going to tell your father, are you?"

"Depends on you, Roy," I shouted back.

Chapter Thirteen

Even with the side of my head hurting as though someone had taken a cut at it with a baseball bat, I was still gloating over my victory over Roy Oates as Mrs. Giordano and I reached the back gate of her yard. I saw the gang over at the ball field, busy with their game of Rotation. Laura and her girl friends were still there watching. How I wished I could have gone right over to tell them what had just happened! Laura would have been so proud of me! She had always been waiting for one of us to stand up to Roy Oates, but I bet she would never have suspected that a little guy like me would have the guts to really do it, to bowl over the big bully, and while he had a gun in his hand, too!

But the story would have to wait. I knew I had a mission to perform first. Funny, at that moment I was probably in greater danger than I'd ever been, but I was no longer scared. I must have lost all my fright during that moment when I realized I had to tackle Roy.

Ding came whizzing past Mrs. Giordano and me while we paused at the gate. I watched him shoot across the field, heading for home. I looked behind me. Roy was still on the back steps of Mrs. Giordano's cottage. I guess he was waiting for us to get away from there before coming out. He was probably still too ashamed to face us.

I turned to Mrs. Giordano. "I think we'd better go see Miss Worthington. She's my friend. She'll help us," I said, studying her dark eyes for some clue as to whether she knew Miss Worthington. I could read nothing there. She just nodded and started to walk beside me as I headed for the parkway.

"We'll take the side streets instead of the avenue," I said, "just in case Early and his men are around. We'll have to make sure they don't spot us."

This time she smiled and patted my head and nodded. We did not say another word to one another the rest of the way. By the time Miss Worthington's house came into view, my head felt as though it would fall off my neck, not only because of Roy's sock to my ear, but because of all the turning and twisting and looking around I did as we walked along, trying to make sure we weren't being followed. I had decided that if I did discover Early tailing me, we would double back and go to my house. The time was near, I figured, when I'd have to tell my parents all about it, anyway.

When we were three houses away from Miss Worthington's, I saw that there was a car parked in front of hers. I stopped in my tracks. Mrs. Giordano threw me a worried, questioning look. "It's not his car," I said, "but there's someone sitting at the wheel. We'd better wait right here or even maybe go back to the corner."

Mrs. Giordano started to retreat, panic on her face.

We went back to the corner and waited. I kept peeking around it every few seconds. I had almost made up my mind to take Mrs. Giordano to my own home when I saw Mrs. True coming out of the yard. She was carrying what looked like a picnic basket. A man came out of the car and helped her in. A moment later they drove away.

"It's all right," I sighed in relief to Mrs. Giordano. We started back toward the house.

As usual the shades were drawn and the windows closed on the second floor. I smiled to myself, thinking, "She's still playing the game. Wait until she sees Mrs. Giordano at the back door with me! She'll die!"

Mrs. Giordano followed me slowly up the stairs. She certainly wasn't acting as though she'd ever been here before. She kept giving me a puzzled look as I kept pounding on the door and rattling the knob and the loud music came pouring out at us from inside. I just kept shrugging and knocking away and hoping Early Winters and his men did not catch up with us before we got into the house.

After a long while, I heard the bolt on the door being slid open and saw the door-knob turn. Miss Worthington stood before us, looking beautiful as ever in a pale green linen sundress. I enjoyed watching the shock shoot up to her face at the sight of us, but I did not keep my eyes on her for long. Quickly, I turned to catch Mrs. Giordano's reaction, but either the lady had never met her son's girl friend before, or she was the best actress in the world, or it was not her son at all who was hiding in that fireplace.

"This is Mrs. Giordano," I said to Miss Worthington.

Both of them just stood there for a while, not seeming to know what to say. I stepped into the apartment, and then Miss Worthington finally said, "Won't you come in, please!"

We went into the kitchen, but still no sign of recognition passed between the two women. Miss Worthington secured the door and invited us into the living room. I smiled as I followed her, because this time I knew what she was up to. She'd sit us down on that divan before the fireplace so that whoever it was she was hiding there could hear every word we said.

Miss Worthington, of course, had already turned off the radio and raised the shades and opened all the windows before she let us into the house. Mrs. Giordano and I sat on the divan, and Miss Worthington stood before us. No one seemed to know what to say. The curtains fluttering noiselessly at the windows, the strange silence that seemed to be everywhere in that room, the thought that in that gigantic fireplace there might be a man, sitting, listening, waiting—everything suddenly seemed weird and unreal to me! What was I doing here alone among these strange people? That man in the fireplace, he might be a real gangster, a killer! And this lady beside me, with her poker face, she could be a slick actress, part of the gang herself. And Miss Worthington—she was hiding him, wasn't she? I felt a chill run down my back.

I heard Miss Worthington clear her throat. The sound almost startled me out of my seat. "Jimmy," she said, "your ear is all bloody. What happened?" She came over and gently inspected my wound.

Funny, that's all it took, just that little kind gesture, and I was once again convinced that she could never be part of anything bad. Nor could poor Mrs. Giordano. I began to scold myself. What was the matter with me, having such dark thoughts about my friends? Where was the courage with which I had toppled Roy?

"It was Roy Oates again," I said, finally answering her question."

"Oh, no!" she said. "I've got you in a terrible mess! Come on out to the kitchen and let me bathe it. We can talk afterwards."

I stood up. "No," I said. "First I've got to warn you and him. Early's closing in on you."

I saw her hands drop to her side. For a moment I thought she'd faint. I looked over at Mrs. Giordano. She was sitting at the edge of the divan, waiting for my next words.

"Miss Worthington, it was Early who drove Roy to do this to me," I began. "I can tell you that—"

"Wait, Jimmy," Miss Worthington interrupted feebly. "You said *him*. What do you mean by *him*?"

"Miss Worthington, you don't have to be afraid of me," I said. "You can trust me. Why do you think I got beat up like this? I wouldn't tell anyone."

"Tell anyone *what*?" Her voice cracked. Her acting was no good now; she was too scared. And, to tell the truth, at that moment so was I, because suddenly I was thinking of the man in the fireplace again. I was the only outsider who knew their secret! Any moment, now, he could come bounding down from there and nail me! I returned to the divan without answering her, my muscles tensed, ready to shoot me out of that house should a foot descend from that chimney.

When I sat down, Mrs. Giordano got up and went over to Miss Worthington. Her eyes were shooting sparks as she took the younger woman's shoulder in her hand. "You know where ees my boy?" she asked in a high-pitched voice.

My eyes shot to the fireplace. Miss Worthington's must have been following mine, for when I looked up at her again, I caught her staring at me in alarm. Mrs. Giordano kept repeating her question. Finally, Miss Worthington let out a long sigh and said, "Please sit down, Mrs. Giordano! We've got a lot of talking to do." She took the older woman's arm and led her back to the divan. "First, though," she said, "I want to hear all about what happened this morning after you left here, Jimmy."

I realized then that there truly must have been someone in that fireplace and that she wanted him to hear my story. To tell the truth, I must have still been gloating over having keeled over Roy Oates, because even though I was still a little scared, I had no trouble in going over every detail for her.

Miss Worthington hardly had time to say, "Oh, how brave!" which was really what I wanted to hear, before Mrs. Giordano was back on her feet, rushing at her, asking again, almost hysterically this time, "You know where ees my boy? You know? You know?"

I did not hear Miss Worthington's answer nor see the expression on her face, for suddenly all my attention went to one spot. The dreaded moment had arrived! I gripped the edge of the divan, frozen there, unable to move a muscle, not even to gulp down the fear that had shot up from my stomach and was stuck in my throat. There they were, slowly making their way down from the flue of that huge fireplace—two men's shoes! The legs followed, in light summer slacks, slowly reaching down toward the floor of the hearth. When the feet finally scraped the stone, the two women whirled around. I heard them gasp, and I sprang to my feet in panic.

The three of us waited and watched as the knees slowly bent and the trunk of a body appeared, and then, finally, a man's head. Crouching low, he stepped out of the hearth and straightened up, his eyes blinking away in the light.

Mrs. Giordano let out a screech. "Evo! Evo!" and ran into the man's arms sobbing. Miss Worthington just stood there, tears beginning to run down the side of her face.

He was a tall, handsome man, with Mrs. Giordano's dark eyes but with sandy hair. I was surprised to see him so well-dressed, in a crisp white summer sport shirt and seersucker trousers. But what impressed me most was how pale he seemed. He, too, had tears in his eyes as he kissed his mother. I had tc swallow hard, but this time it was not from fear but because of mixed joy and sadness.

There was nothing in the face of Evo Montella that would ever frighten anyone. When he smiled at his mother and then over at Miss Worthington, he seemed the nicest guy I'd ever seen. I kept thinking of him cooped up in this apartment for almost a year, running to hide in that fireplace whenever anyone came to call. It must have been hell! A good thing he had Miss Worthington. They were in love, all right! I could tell from the way he was looking at her over his mother's shoulders. They were a beautiful couple, like you'd see in the movies. They would have been married by now, I bet, if he had been free.

I saw him coming toward me. He held out his hand. "You're a great kid!" he said. "And I want to thank you for being so nice to my mother." He shook my hand, and I felt right off I was going to like him. "And you've got lots of guts, too, Jimmy," he added. His words made me feel all warm inside.

I looked at Miss Worthington, and I could see her face getting all worried again. I guess Evo saw it, too, because he patted me on the shoulder, then went over to take her hand. "It's all right, Bessie," he said. "This kid's made me see something today." He put his arm around her waist and held her tight. Then he reached over and with his other arm hugged his mother. "Oh, God, how nice it is to be out in the open again! Free!" He let out a long sigh and hugged them both closer.

"Yep," he said after a while, "I guess I knew it all along, but it took Jimmy here to drive it home to me. Just like he found the guts to stand up to that bully of a Roy, I've got to find the guts to face up to reality. After all, I had nothing to do with the killing. I was just there." He let go of his mother and his sweetheart. "Bessie," he said, "would you please look up the number of the police department. I'm going to give myself up."

Both women looked horrified.

"It's the only way," he said. "All I did wrong was to drive that truck. I had no idea they were setting out to hijack another bootlegger. I'll tell the truth—take what's coming to me. They'll understand. It's the best way."

"No, Evo, no!" his mother called out.

"Are you forgetting about Winters?" Miss Worthington asked. She looked ready to cry. "Are you forgetting why you've been hiding like this? That gang won't ever let you testify. They'll kill you first!" She began to sob softly.

He put his arm around her. "Please," he said gently, "don't cry. I've caused you enough pain already. The police will protect us. You'll see. The truth is best, Bessie, you know that."

Now it was his mother who began to cry, only her crying was almost a howl. Miss Worthington became alarmed and began to run around the room closing windows. "Oh, God, the whole neighborhood will hear us!" she said.

In the midst of all this, a loud knocking from the direction of the back door reached us. All of us became instantly quiet. The rapping rang out again, fearsome in the silent house. We pussy-footed across the living room, stopping at the doorway that opened into the kitchen.

Then a voice: "All right! We know you're in there!"

Terror struck all four of our faces at once as we stood

staring across the kitchen at the rear door. It was Early Winters! No one dared to move. I felt my heart pound so strong that my chest ached.

"Okay, have it your way!" Early bellowed. There was a loud thud and the door shuddered. Miss Worthington looked at Evo in alarm and pointed toward the fireplace as we retreated a couple of steps back into the living room.

Evo shook his head. His mother came over to him, whimpering in Italian. I could tell from her motions she was telling him to get back into that fireplace. Another thud against the door! This time we heard something crack. Miss Worthington grasped Evo's arm and tried to pull him toward the fireplace.

There was another crash, and I knew at once it was too late. In an instant, Early Winters and his pal were standing at the living room doorway, guns drawn. Just behind them, his head hanging in shame, was Roy Oates.

"Okay, Evo," Early said, "now let's all just sit down and talk things over. We're not here to hurt anyone." He smiled that ugly, evil smile of his that made my skin crawl. He put his revolver back in the holster under his jacket, but his henchman kept his gun trained on us all the while. Early led us back into the living room and motioned Evo to sit on the divan between Miss Worthington and his mother. He made me sit in the armchair to the right of the divan, and Roy, whose eyes still hadn't come up off the floor, in the chair to the left, facing me.

"Now," Early said, "I can understand you hiding from

the police, Evo. But why from me? Why from your friends?" Again he gave that smile with which he was trying so hard to seem friendly, but which only made him look like a vicious, snarling boxer dog.

Evo shrugged his shoulders. "Just playing it safe," he said.

"It's dumb! Dumb!" Early said in a raspy whisper. "All this time lost. You could have been away from here, safe and sound somewhere. Really safe!"

Evo said nothing. I could see his eyes moving all around the room, sizing up the situation. His mind was busy, I could tell. Early Winters was too wound up in his own speech to notice. But Evo was planning, waiting for the right moment. He had no intention of having Winters take him so easily. The brave expression on his face made it easy for me to forget all danger. I knew if he made a move, I'd be ready to help.

"You've got to learn to trust your friends more, Evo," Winters went on, shaking his head. "Now, if you come along with us, we'll make sure you get settled in a nice, peaceful spot. Later we can send for your mother and your sweetheart here. You'll be free and safe and peaceful."

"Yeah. That's what they say about the dead," Evo answered.

Early's horrid smile made my blood run cold again. "Only if you insist on staying here, will you have to worry about death," he said. "Now, smarten up, kid! We're trying to do you a favor. We could take care of you right here, if that's what we wanted to do, and right now!"

The tone of Early's words made me shiver, but Evo didn't seem to be scared at all. He straightened up and looked right at Early. "You know damn well you wouldn't kill me right here. Early Winters' too clever for that. He wouldn't risk taking the rap himself for the killing of a two-bit car driver."

Mrs. Giordano was getting very nervous. She reached into her pocket and pulled out her rosary and began to pray again. Early watched her for a while. "You should have some of your mother's faith," he said. "Faith in your friends. How do you expect to get out of here if you don't trust *somebody*?"

He walked away and began pacing in front of the fireplace. His buddy, who had been standing back there with his gun playing upon us, now moved forward to stand between where Roy and I were sitting.

For the first time since coming into the house, Roy looked up. Our eyes met, and he quickly looked away and then down at the floor by his feet again. "He's ashamed," I thought, "ashamed to be considered part of this gangster's team. Sure, he's a bully, but he's not really that bad! He's probably worrying right now about what my father will do when he finds out about all this and whether he'll ever be allowed to work in the garage again. He'd rather be what my father is than have all the evil power of an Early Winters or even an Al Capone. He's one of us! He was just scared, that's why he sided with those thugs! I looked up at him and kept staring and staring, hoping our eyes would meet once more. I had a message to get to him.

Winters came back to the divan. This time he talked to Miss Worthington. "You try to make him understand, miss! We're not trying to hurt him. He's one of us, and we want to help him."

Miss Worthington nodded, but her mind seemed miles away. She never did answer Early, nor did she say a word to Evo. Winters threw up his hands and went back to his pacing. His pal stood there before us, his gun ready should any of us make a move.

Finally, Roy was looking right at me. I winked, trying to tell him there were no hard feelings. He winked back. I continued to stare at him. After a while he caught on that I was trying to tell him something. My eyes still on him, I nodded toward Early's henchman, who was still standing between us but who was becoming uneasy now, shifting his weight from one foot to the other. Roy nodded back, very slightly, but enough to tell me that we were in touch.

We continued to follow one another's eyes for quite a while. When I was sure the gunman was looking the other way, I dropped my hands to my lap and then, clenching my fists, tapped the sides of my knees. I saw Roy nod. Had he really understood my signal?

The man with the gun was becoming very restless now, beginning to stretch his neck and to look around the room more and more. I kept my eyes on Roy and he kept his on mine. I waited for the right moment, then dropped my right shoulder and threw it forward, the way you would in throwing a football tackle. Roy answered with a wink. When he saw Early's man looking away again, he pointed with his finger, first to me, then to himself, and then punched the palm of his left hand silently with his right.

Roy had understood, all right, and Roy was ready! Yes, he was ready to redeem himself. An icy shudder ran down my back that made me straighten up in my chair. I guess Roy thought I was getting ready to make my move, because I saw him edge forward in his seat and tense up, ready to spring. But things weren't that easy. There were others to worry about. Roy and I could hit that man from both sides, but that gun might go off and hit one of our friends on the divan. And, then, there was Early Winters, up front with a gun in his holster which he could produce in a second.

Early came back to Evo again. "Tell me, kid, what do I have to do to convince you? We just want you where the police can't find you, that's all. If you've got a better idea, you tell me how you want it done."

"Look, Early," Evo answered, looking him square in the eye, "you're not kidding *me*! You know darn well you won't feel safe till I'm six feet under. Now, I'm gonna leave this place, whether you like it or not. And *I'm* gonna choose the time! So you might just as well leave now."

I never saw so much hate as flashed up in Early Winters' face. His voice trembled with anger as he answered. "Don't push me, kid! And don't kid yourself! I'll take care of you right here if I have to!"

Evo didn't move. I know how he would have loved to go after that evil man with his bare hands, but he knew the odds were against him. This was just not the time.

Evo's mother, frightened by Early's threats, had stopped saying her rosary and was sobbing again. Suddenly, she stood up. Early's man became excited by her move and stepped forward, his gun menacing. Her eyes flashed at the sight of it. "*Assassini*!" she screeched in Italian, and she lashed out at the man with her rosary beads. He let out a yelp of pain as the beads tangled around his hands and the gun fell to the floor.

My eyes met Roy's. At the same instant both of us were off our feet, sailing toward our target. Early's man came down with a thud as both our tackles hit him, one above and one below the knees. Roy's weight and power was greater than mine so that both of them landed on me. I wriggled myself free and hurried to sit on the man's legs. Roy was already sitting on his stomach and pounding away at him with his fists.

Even in all this excitement, Evo's words reached me. "All right, Early, I'll take this." I glanced around for just a second, long enough to discover that Evo had recovered the gun Mrs. Giordano had knocked out of the gunman's hand and that he was now covering Early Winters with it while reaching into the gangster's holster to remove the other gun.

"Okay, boys, you can let him up now," Evo said a few moments later. "I've got them both covered."

Roy and I rose to our feet. The bewildered henchman lay on the floor. "Okay, over on your belly!" Evo called to him. "And you, Early, right down here on the floor beside him! Move! On your belly!"

"I'll get you for this, Montella! You must be crazy to think you can get away with this!" Early said as he obeyed.

"Yeah, okay. Let me worry about that," Evo said, pointing both guns at them. "Right now, Bessie, go to that phone and call the police!"

Miss Worthington ran to the kitchen to place the call. Mrs. Giordano sat on the divan and began to say her rosary again. I looked at Roy. He had a big grin on his face. He winked when he caught me looking at him. I winked back. It was a nice feeling. Evo stood over the two gangsters, very serious, not saying a word, not even when Miss Worthington came back into the room to tell us the police were on their way.

A few minutes later we heard the sirens sound and then the banging of the police car doors in the street below. "I'll get you for this, don't ever forget!" Early Winters said.

"It's worth the chance," Evo said calmly. "I should have gone to the police in the first place."

Miss Worthington came to his side and put her head on his shoulders, and he turned and kissed her on the cheek. I looked at Roy. He was taking it all in, grinning away. Again he winked at me and then nodded, as if to say that everything was turning out just fine.

Chapter Fourteen

There's a FOR SALE sign now on the little white cottage in left field. Not a day goes by that I don't find myself looking away for a moment from our game toward the gate to Mrs. Giordano's yard, expecting to see her standing there watching us. My little brother still goes down and sits against the picket fence, not understanding why she does not come out. I know I should be proud and happy over the way things turned out, but I can't hold back the sadness as I notice how the weeds have taken over in the gardens she used to tend so lovingly.

And when I go to the library now, the same sadness follows me, because another lady sits behind the circulation desk in Miss Worthington's place, and though she's pleasant enough, I long to hear Miss Worthington's light step following me to the stacks and her musical whisper behind me, guiding. "That's a good one, Jimmy! You'll like it. A bit advanced, but I think you can manage it." Sometimes I actually have to blink a tear away as I remember and as I realize that somewhere out there in the world I have a friend whom I shall never see again.

Yet, the story has a happy ending. Evo Montella gave himself up to the police that afternoon, and they arrested Early Winters and his partner. Mrs. Montella—or Mrs. Giordano as I prefer to remember her—and Miss Worthington were also taken away by the police, for their own protection. Roy and I were taken home to our parents.

I've never seen my father more proud of anyone than he was of me as he listened to the detectives tell the story of what Roy and I had done. That pride has stayed with him, too. I can still feel it in the way he treats me. Even when he has to scold me for something I have done wrong, I can feel it there. He doesn't get on my back for reading too much anymore, either. Sometimes he even asks me about the book I've been reading and listens with interest, particularly when it's about ancient history. I guess you could say my father and I have been getting much closer to one another since that day.

In the neighborhood, Roy and I really became heroes. Everybody wanted to hear our story, and I've got to admit I really enjoyed telling it, especially when Laura Russo was listening. A few times I overheard her telling it to some of her girl friends, and I guess that's when my pride was strongest of all.

But the way Roy Oates acted was a little strange. You'd have thought the old bully would have gone bragging all over the place, but instead he seemed to become a different person. As a matter of fact, he almost stopped playing with our gang completely. He became very serious and spent almost all his spare time working in my father's garage. "That boy sure grew up in a hurry!" I heard my father say to his father one day.

I never told anyone, not even my parents, of Roy's cooperation with Early Winters, and I made Ding swear never to tell of what had gone on in Mrs. Giordano's cellar when Roy had tried to hold us prisoners. I figured Roy had learned his lesson and that he'd proven his loyalty to us afterwards.

Evo Montella was brave enough to testify against Early Winters. Early was given a long jail term for masterminding a highjacking that led to the death of two of his own men and two G-men. Evo was given a deferred sentence, and he and Miss Worthington and Mrs. Giordano were given new names and new identities and set up in some community somewhere. I heard later from a detective who came to visit my father that Evo and Miss Worthington had been married while the trial was still going on. He also told us we'd never hear from them again, for Early and his men would go on hunting for them and so their whereabouts must always remain secret.

The detective had a parcel for me from Miss Worthington. When I opened it, I found it was a book, the most beautiful book I've ever seen. It was bound in brown leather with great engravings all over it, and the edges of the pages were gilded. I turned it to look at the name. *The Alhambra* by Washington Irving! This time I couldn't fight back the tears. I opened it. On the flyleaf I read: "TO MY BRAVE LITTLE FRIEND, JIMMY, WITH LOVE—Bessie Worthington." I had to run upstairs to my room so that the others would not see me cry.

I thumb through the book often now, and I think of the three of them, picturing them in another little white cottage by a ball field somewhere in this big country of ours. Their name is probably Smith or Campbell or something. Someday they'll probably have a little boy of their own, and Mrs. Giordano can watch proudly as her son teaches him how to hit a ball. I'll never see them and I'll never really know, but I'll love them all always.

The Author

Remus F. Caroselli grew up in a neighborhood in Providence, Rhode Island, like the one he describes in *The Mystery Cottage in Left Field.* He is a member of the American Chemical Society and is presently on the Research Advisory Board of the Textile Research Institute. A research chemist and director for many years, he has more than thirty patents in the field of textile technology. The author of technical articles, he makes his debut as a novelist with this book. Mr. Caroselli is active in many civic affairs in Narragansett, Rhode Island, where he now lives.